Hang on in there, Shelley

Hang on in there, Shelley

by Kate Saksena

BLOOMSBURY
CHILDREN'S
BOOKS

**BLOOMSBURY
CHILDREN'S
BOOKS**

Copyright © 2003 by Kate Saksena

Published by Bloomsbury, New York and London
Distributed to the trade by Holtzbrinck Publishers

Library of Congress Cataloging-in-Publication Data:
Saksena, Kate.
Hang on in there, Shelley / by Kate Saksena.
p. cm.
Summary: Living in London, fourteen-year-old Shelley writes letters to a pop star which describe her life with friends and family, including her divorced alcoholic mother, and struggles with a school bully.
ISBN 1-58234-822-7 (alk. paper)
[1. Family Problems—Fiction. 2. Alcoholism—Fiction. 3. Bullies—Fiction.
4. School—Fiction. 5. Racially mixed people—Fiction. 6. Letters—Fiction. 7. London (England)—Fiction. 8. England—Fiction.] I. Title.
PZ7.S14398 Han 2003
[E]—dc21
2002027819

First U.S. Edition 2003
Printed in Great Britain

1 3 5 7 9 10 8 6 4 2

Bloomsbury USA Children's Books
175 Fifth Avenue
New York, New York 10010

For my daughter

TELL ME NO LIE

Tell me no lie
Honesty
Integrity
Make a man
Feel like he's free

August 15

Dear Ziggy,
Today is my birthday, I'm 14. I've been a fan of Arctic Zoo for two years now. My mum gave me your new album and my Auntie Zandra sent away to your fan club for some posters and magazines. They were my best presents ever. I've now got a poster of you on my bedroom wall and I've read *all* the magazines already, including the long interview you did with Dr X. I was so impressed with what you said. It sounds like your family is a bit like mine – I found that reassuring. But what I liked best was what you said about being honest with yourself. Do you remember? You said it wasn't *always* a good idea to be honest with everyone

else but you must be honest with yourself and with at least one person you really trust. You said it again in *Tell me no lie*. I really like that track. This made me think and I decided to write an honest account of my life and try to keep it up for a whole year. I hope you don't mind but I've decided I'm going to write this for you, because I feel I can trust you.

This way, I can be really honest. I don't think I could in a diary. I'd be afraid my mum would read it, so I'd always be careful about what I wrote. That's not honesty. By writing to you, I am sending my thoughts to someone I can really be honest with.

It's probably a silly idea and I know you must get thousands of letters and you'll have a secretary to read them. I thought about that and I don't mind too much but I'd prefer it if you read them. Please let me know if you do. OK, here goes. My name is Shelley. I'm 14. I'm an Arctic Zoo fan. I'm not very tall, I'm skinny, I have dark brown hair which I usually wear in little plaits. I have a white mum and a black dad which makes me mixed race – which is sometimes great and sometimes confusing. It sometimes makes me feel I don't really belong anywhere, but that's only in my bad moments. I've got an eight-year-old brother called Jake. We live with our mum in a flat in

South London. We only moved here three weeks ago. It's quite a nice flat – there's a park next door – but it can get noisy sometimes. My dad doesn't live with us. He lives about a mile away with his new girlfriend, Marilyn. I've got two nans, four aunts, two uncles and four cousins – so my family is quite big – but some of them live quite a long way away. And that's about it as far as my family's concerned. I can't really tell you about my school because I haven't got one right now. I used to go to Singleton County – but now that we've moved it's too far to travel. I'm pleased, I didn't like it very much. I'll be starting a new school – Knighton Girls – in a couple of weeks.

I'm trying not to think about that at the moment. It's still the summer holidays. Now I think I've reached the difficult bit. I could go on about school or the weather or our flat or I could try to describe honestly the first three weeks of my holiday. If these letters are going to mean anything then I've got to take a deep breath and explain a few things about my family.

I'll start with my mum. I really love her but sometimes she's very difficult to love. She's 30. She's got long blonde hair (dyed) and a pretty face. She used to be quite slim but she's put on a bit of weight recently.

I'm not sure she really recognises this because she still wears the same clothes and some of them are a bit tight now. Her name is Liz. She used to be a secretary in a printing company but last year she got the sack. They told her they were 'downsizing' the company (whatever that means) but I think they got fed up with the amount of time she had off work.

You see (and I'm finding this difficult to write) my mum gets depressed quite often and when she's depressed she drinks too much. Last year, before she got the sack, there were quite a few mornings when she got me to phone in to say she had food poisoning or a migraine.

So, the truth is, she lost her job. Then she couldn't pay the mortgage on our house. Dad paid it for a while – he works for a computer company – but now Marilyn's pregnant and they're buying a house, so he can't afford to pay all our bills as well.

Mum sold our old place and we lived with my nan for a few months until this flat came up and, as I said, we moved in at the beginning of the holidays. The first week was great. Mum was enthusiastic and the whole family came and helped paint all the rooms. I share a bedroom with Jake. He's got the top bunk and I've got the bottom. We decided to paint our room bright green. It looks really cheerful and my Auntie Zandra made us some purple-and-green-check curtains.

The place looks nice now – though I miss having a garden and I don't like all the stairs. We're on the third floor!

It was the second week that things started to go wrong. Mum's been looking for a job, but each time she gets turned down she gets very upset. On the Monday I'd taken Jake to the library – he listened to the storyteller who was there and I used the computer. Then we went to the park for a while on the way home. We got back in time for children's television and Jake watched it while I went to make some toast.

Mum came in. She looked awful.

'What the hell are you doing?' she shouted at me and flung the toast on the floor.

'Calm down, Mum,' I said, trying to be calm myself.

'Don't tell me what to do,' she screamed.

'What's the matter?' I asked her.

'Nothing's the matter with me,' she shouted. 'It's you!'

'I'm only making some toast!' I said.

'You're always making toast,' she was shouting really loud now. 'You selfish little cow, you're always making food or drinks for yourself, reading to yourself, doing things on your own. What about Jake and me?'

I knew nothing would shut her up. I could smell the alcohol on her now.

'I've made toast for Jake,' I said. 'And I'll make some for you, if you want.'

'No. Don't you worry about me. Just you keep on with your self-centred ways and ignore me. I'm only your mother.'

With that she burst into tears. I was relieved. Usually when she starts crying it means she's finished shouting. I put my arm round her and hugged her. She was sobbing and saying how sorry she was and how much she loved me. I managed to get her to her bedroom and soon she was fast asleep. So Jake and I had a quiet evening.

Anyway, that week was pretty awful, but the weather was fine so Jake and I spent time in the park or in the library or visiting Auntie Zandra or Nan. Then on Saturday Mum told us she wanted us all to do something together. She seemed in a good mood so we went to Greenwich. We had a lovely day. We visited the observatory and the market and ate sandwiches in the park. I haven't seen Jake or Mum so happy for ages. She bought him a balloon and he was ridiculously pleased with it. When we got home, Mum said she had to slip down to her friend, Eileen's, to return something. We all knew it wasn't true. She didn't come back until 4 o'clock the next morning. She made such a noise that I woke up. I thought she'd fallen over in the hall so I peeped out of the door to see. She saw me and started swearing at me and accusing me of spying on her.

'You're always checking up on me, and spying, and watching. You always look so disapproving! Just stop it. Don't look at me!'

I thought it would make things worse if I said anything so I went back to our room and shut the door. I think Jake was awake. He didn't say anything but the silence somehow felt like a listening kind of silence. It's continued like that ever since. I've tried to take Jake out every day – that way we don't get into trouble for waking her up or making too much noise.

You can see that it hasn't been a brilliant holiday so far. Until today. Today, everything's going to change because I've got your album to play, your poster to look at and I've decided to write you these letters.

I'm feeling really hopeful that you'll reply. I must go now. My nan has arrived with a birthday cake and a present. Things really are looking up!

Lots of love,
Shelley

Hang on in there,
Shelley. ·

Ziggy

Shelley Wright
16 Waterstone House
London SE6
Inghilterra

POSTCARD

Another postcard, another town
Another chance for them to put me down
But they'll fail.
'Cos I've got you on my side

September 1

Dear Ziggy,
I'm so happy. I'm over the moon. I'm thrilled. You did write to me – and from Italy too! Thank you, thank you, thank you. You've no idea how much it cheered me up.

I last wrote to you on my birthday. Well, it was a great birthday. We had a lovely tea and then went to the cinema to see *Antz*. The following day Jake and I went to my dad's. He told me he'd got me a present that I'd really like. Dad and Marilyn have really good taste in clothes so I thought it might be some trainers or a leather jacket or something. When Jake and I arrived the two of them were obviously really excited about this present.

15

'It's not wrapped,' said my dad.

I looked around the room.

'Where is it?' I asked.

'It's in the dining room,' said Marilyn.

'But you've got to shut your eyes,' said Dad and grabbed my hand.

Marilyn grabbed Jake's and they made a big fuss about us keeping our eyes shut tight. Then they led us into the dining room and said, 'Open.'

I think I screamed. I was so excited. It was a computer! I could not believe it. I hugged them both. Jake was actually jumping up and down, he was so excited. It was a PC with all the bits – CD-ROM, printer, speakers . . .

'It's not brand new,' explained Dad. 'But it's just the job for you two to use.'

We spent the rest of the day playing about with it and trying things out. You can see from this letter – from now on I'm typing everything.

In the evening, Dad drove us home and we carried all the computer bits into our bedroom. Dad set it all up on a table. It fitted in just fine. We'd just got it all finished and were standing admiring it when we heard the front door slam. Mum was home. She came in and stared at us.

'Come to play happy families, have you?' she said in a nasty tone.

'No, Liz. I just brought the kids home. I'll go now,' replied Dad.

'What on earth is that?' she asked, pointing at the computer. She was swaying and slurring her words.

'It's a present,' said Dad.

There was a dangerous silence. Then she started shouting.

'You're just trying to bribe them aren't you? You think if you buy them things like that they'll want to leave me and live with you. I know how your mind works.'

Jake started crying and put his hands over his ears. I put my arm round him.

'For God's sake, Liz, you're upsetting Jake. You know he doesn't like you shouting!' said Dad.

'Don't tell me what *my* son likes or dislikes! This is my flat. You don't have any rights here.'

'I just want you to calm down!' Dad was getting exasperated.

'Calm down! Why should I? You come here acting Father Christmas with this expensive present. It must have cost a fortune. It would have been more help if you'd given me some cash to feed and clothe them instead of buying this!'

'Liz, that's not fair. I do help with the bills. And this didn't cost a lot. A company was upgrading and this one was going spare. You know how much Shelley likes computers!'

'Shelley likes computers,' she repeated in a mocking voice. 'The trouble is, Ben, you think Shelley's a perfect angel and she isn't. She's—'

At this point I couldn't stand it anymore. I grabbed Jake and went into the kitchen and shut the door. We heard some more shouting, then Dad left. Jake was still sobbing. I've got used to Mum's rantings but Jake still gets really upset – that's what makes me angry with her.

Jake. I'll tell you a bit about Jake. He looks a lot like me – but I don't think he is like me in character. Jake is very quiet and shy. He's more than shy, he's quite nervous. Ever since I can remember I've looked after Jake – put him to bed, woken him up, taken him to school – so I suppose we're quite close. I think we're a bit unusual. Most girls of my age with eight-year-old brothers fight with them all of the time. We don't fight very often, but I suppose that's because Jake isn't the type to argue. I worry about Jake.

Anyway, after a while Mum came into the kitchen.

She was crying (as usual after she's been horrible) and she hugged us and told us how much she loved us and how sorry she was that she always argued with Dad when she saw him.

Since then, Jake and I have had a lot of fun with the computer. We've designed all sorts of things, played a few games, written stories and letters and found out about all sorts of things from the CD-ROMs Dad's given us. It's been great and Jake's got really confident about using it.

On the second day we had the computer we got completely confused. So we went to the library to see if there was a handbook to help us. Jake was choosing a reading book and I was searching for a handbook. There was a librarian looking at me very suspiciously. She's tall and thin and quite old. She looks *very* stern.

'Are you looking for something?' she asked.

'Yes,' I said, but she made me nervous.

'Are you sure you aren't just messing about?'

'Oh no. I want a handbook for my computer.'

'They all come with handbooks!' she said.

'Only if they're new!' I said. 'Mine isn't new so there's no book and I'm stuck.'

Somehow, she suddenly seemed to believe me. I explained the problem and she told me there wasn't a handbook on the shelves but she had the same computer in her office. She took me into the office, showed me how to sort out the problem and photocopied some pages from her own handbook for me.

I discovered she wasn't stern at all. Since then we often go to the library to ask for her help or talk to her. Her name is Dorothy Graham. She claims we're much more skilled using the computer than she is now!

Yesterday, my nan came round. She had a go at Mum because she hasn't bought us our uniform for the beginning of term. Mum started crying and ran out of the flat. Nan took us shopping. When we got home I put on the whole lot to see what I looked like. It's green! Green sweatshirt, green skirt and white shirt. I look like a tree in it, like one of those yew trees they make shapes from. She's even bought some new shoes and tights.

I had a moment of real panic when we went into the shoe shop. Nan wanted to buy some seriously, seriously dreadful shoes for me.

'I can't wear those, Nan!' I objected.

'Why on earth not? They look just the job for school,' Nan insisted.

They were very flat, strangely shaped lace-up

shoes. The only people who wear shoes like that are incredibly old.

'Nan,' I said, 'these shoes are too old even for you! There's an age restriction on them. Look, inside it says "Not to be worn by persons younger than 85".'

Nan laughed but was not convinced.

I pointed to some quite acceptable shoes nearby. There was a girl and her mother looking at them.

'Look, she's about my age. If she can wear those to school, so can I!'

'Don't be silly, Shelley, they're much too high!' said Nan. But within a few seconds she'd moved in on the girl and her mother and had engaged them in conversation. That's what my nan's like. She talks to everyone! I swear that within a few minutes she manages not only to tell our family's life history but also to find out the intimate details of the other person's daily life.

At moments like this, usually I pretend she's not with me but, in fact, this time it worked in my favour. The girl went to Knighton School and both she and her mum assured Nan that the shoes were allowed and all the girls wore them. I was so relieved. I smiled at the girl and thanked her for persuading Nan. She smiled back. She looked nice. I hope they're all going to be like her.

So, I'm all set for the term. I'm getting nervous now! A new school. I don't know anyone there – but they'll all know each other.

I know Jake's nervous too. The good thing is, his school is on the same road as mine so I'll be able to walk to school and back with him.

I'm trying to calm my nerves by playing your album. I find *Magic* a very soothing track. It reminds me of a calm sea!

Please write again,
Lots of love,
Shelley

Good luck,
Shelley.

Ziggy

Shelley Wright
16 Waterstone House
London SE6

SCHOOLDAZE

Lost in a big haze
Those early school daze
Shuttered, watchful,
On the edge of life

September 15

Dear Ziggy,
I really can't believe you've sent another postcard. It's given me the confidence to continue my 'honesty letters'. Thank you very much! Such a lot has happened in the past two weeks, I'm not sure where to start – but I suppose it has to be school.

Jake and I began our new schools last week. Jake was really nervous that morning. Mum had said she'd go to school with him that first day – but she was still in bed when we left. I stayed with Jake as long as I could and before I left I asked a tall boy to look after him – but I still felt bad as I walked out of the gate. When I looked back, Jake looked so small and frightened and alone – like a baby rabbit.

I rushed over to my school and presented myself to the office. A secretary made a phone call and a woman came to introduce herself to me. Her name is Mrs Doherty. She's small and quite plump – about 50 years old. She's got grey hair cut very short and she wears short skirts and jumpers in really bright colours. She came over to me that first day with a big smile.

'Hello, you must be Shelley. I'm your Head of Year. Welcome to your new school.'

She marched me off and I had to walk very fast to keep up with her. She told me we were on our way to my new class. After passing through endless corridors she stopped at a classroom door.

'Well, this is it, Shelley,' she said and smiled again. 'A word of advice – smile at everyone, be very friendly but keep a low profile for three weeks. Take it all slowly!'

With that she opened the classroom door and I had my first glimpse of 10M. There were 26 of them, sitting very quietly – all staring at *me*! I was introduced to my new form tutor Miss McKenzie. She was a bit of a surprise. She was young, black, and very pretty. There hadn't been teachers like her at my old school!

I sat down near the front and Miss McKenzie asked the girl next to me to look after me. Her name was Hazel and she had hazel eyes. I took my new Head of Year's advice. I was friendly and smiled at everyone. Nearly all of them were friendly to me – but there was a girl called Janice and her friends Charlene and Olivia who seemed to think they were very superior. I was so relieved when that day was over. It was such a strain trying to remember names, rooms, times, and keep up with everyone else.

I rushed across the road at the end of school to find Jake. He was standing outside with the same big boy.

'I've looked after him, like you asked,' said the boy and, obviously relieved to finish his duty, ran off. Jake said his day had been all right, and we compared notes on our way home.

The following day was not quite so pleasant. I arrived in our classroom first thing. Hazel was not there yet – but those three, Olivia, Charlene and Janice, were. I put my bag down on the desk I'd been at the previous day.

'There's something different about the classroom today,' I heard Janice say in an overloud voice.

'It's more crowded!' Charlene said.

'It smells different too,' Olivia joined in.

I wasn't sure what to do. The other girls had gone quiet. They were watching and waiting. I had to decide quickly whether or not to respond to these comments. I decided it would probably be foolish. They were secure and sure of themselves, I was not. They had friends, I did not. Everyone knew them, no one knew me. Low profile, I thought, and turned to the trio smiling very brightly.

'It's the new paint,' I said, still smiling, and busied myself with my books, trying to hide my shaking hands. The tension disappeared in the class and everyone began to talk again. Hazel arrived and I chatted to her.

I watched those three very carefully that day. They obviously considered themselves much more sophisticated than the rest of us. All three had elaborate hair-styles, make-up and beautifully painted nails. Their skirts were shorter than everyone else's and their heels were higher. They sniggered about boys most of the time and disappeared every so often. When they returned they smelt of smoke.

However, they didn't say anything else to me. At the end of school I found Jake with the big boy again.

'What's he like?' I asked Jake as the boy ran off.

'He's OK. Everyone seems to be scared of him!'

'He's not nasty to you is he?' I asked, worried that I'd put Jake into the hands of some bully.

'No, he's really kind. I like him. It's just—'

'Just what?' I demanded, a bit worried.

'Well, I don't think he's very bright!' said Jake in a whisper.

'Maybe you can help him then,' I suggested.

At home that evening things were a bit bleak. Mum had a friend round when we got home. Her name is Eileen. The living room was littered with bottles and overflowing ashtrays.

'Hello my lovelies, how was school?' said Mum when we walked in. She hugged us both too tightly and breathed alcohol and cigarettes all over us.

'We'll go and have a drink,' I said, pulling Jake towards the kitchen.

'No, no,' said Mum. 'I'll go and get you a drink. You sit down and talk to Eileen.'

She staggered out and we heard crashing in the kitchen. Eileen just sat and giggled. I could see Jake beginning to get tearful. I went to see what Mum was doing. She'd fallen over. The kitchen was very small and she'd knocked a chair over. She was covered in milk and the bottle lay broken beside her.

'Are you all right?' I asked and began to pull her up.

'Leave me alone. I can manage,' she said, pushing me away.

I got a dustpan and brush and started to clear up the broken glass. She tried to stand up but slipped again and cut her hand.

'You're hurt,' I said, looking at her hand. 'You need to wash it and put on a plaster.'

'I know what to do, thank you,' she said, snarling. 'I don't need a 13-year-old to tell me how to treat a cut.'

I wanted to shout at her that I was 14 but thought better of it.

I tried to pull her up but she shrugged me off and crawled her way through the broken glass. I'm sure she must have cut herself again. I heard her go into the bathroom, so I quickly cleared everything up, made a drink and found some biscuits. I called Jake and we went into our bedroom, away from the smell and her awful friend Eileen. I could hear Mum being sick. It's a good job we haven't got a lock on the bathroom door. An hour later, I found her asleep on the floor. Jake and I managed to get her to her room. We thought we'd have to put up with Eileen all night but once she'd drunk everything in the house she left to find more.

The third day at school things were even worse. In the morning the Trio greeted me.

'I'm feeling claustrophobic, all of a sudden,' said Janice.

'It's the overcrowding,' said Olivia.

'It's that funny fishy smell again,' said Charlene.

I braced myself. What to do? If I ignored them, they'd just keep on doing this. Besides, after the horrible evening I'd had I was in no mood to put up with their stupid remarks.

I went up to the three of them.

'Janice, if you have a problem with claustrophobia, you should see a psychiatrist!' I said to her.

The class was silent. Everyone watched. There was a sense of excitement and menace in the room. Janice stared at me, her eyes widening in anger. Her two mates stared at her.

'Shut your nasty little mouth,' snarled Janice.

'I was only concerned for your health,' I said, smiling much too broadly.

'I don't want your concern!' she said. She got off her desk and stood facing me. We were about the same height but she was much, much bigger than me. Her eyes gleamed in anger and I think she was about to hit me. But right then, Miss McKenzie walked in.

'Good morning, girls. Everyone in their seats, please.'

I don't know if Miss McKenzie saw what was happening. I do know that everyone suddenly busied themselves and Janice and I moved away from each other.

The rest of the day was strange. Some of the other girls, including Hazel, warned me that Janice was best avoided. And during maths, Charlene knocked my pencil case onto the floor as she went past. When I bent down to pick it up, she leaned down and hissed, 'Don't try to be clever, new girl.'

The day ended well. Mum had cleaned everything and made us a lovely tea and promised not to see Eileen again. So, at least things are looking up at home.

Write to me again, please,
Shelley

Hang on in there,
Shelley

Love Ziggy

Shelley Wright
16 Waterstone House
London SE6

HI-TEC

Pushing buttons
Clicking mice
Tapping keys
She's a Hi-Tec kid
In a Hi-Tec world

October 1

Dear Ziggy,

I'm sure you have no idea how much confidence it gives me, knowing that you get my letters and send me your cards. It keeps me going even when things are difficult.

Well, as you probably imagined the situation with the Trio got nasty again. After a few days of nothing more than dirty looks, things took a turn for the worse.

It was break and we were all in the classroom. The Trio came in reeking of smoke and making a big fuss because the Deputy Head had nearly caught them smoking.

'I think someone grassed us up,' said Janice accusingly.

'So do I!' Charlene agreed. 'How else did she know where to look?'

They muttered and cursed and then all three of them stared at me.

'You know,' said Janice, in her loud, mean voice, 'last year, no one grassed us up. So what's changed this year?'

'Well, I can only think of one thing,' said Olivia pointedly.

I could feel all eyes on me now and I could feel myself getting angry. How dare they accuse me! I turned in my seat to face them head on.

'I hope you're not suggesting that I grassed on you!' I said.

'Well,' said Janice. 'How else do you explain it?'

'I imagine the teachers know where everyone goes to smoke anyway!'

'And where is that?' asked Olivia in a sly tone.

'I don't really know,' I said. 'I don't smoke and I don't know where things are in the school yet.'

'But as soon as you find out you'll let one of the teachers know, I bet!' said Janice, her lip curling.

'No. I couldn't care less whether you smoke or not.'

'That's good, because if we thought it was you…'
she just left the threat hanging unfinished in the air.

'Yes,' I replied. 'What would you do?'

Janice wasn't very quick, and she was a bit surprised at the question.

'We'd feel that we should report some of your activities to Miss McKenzie!' answered Olivia.

'Like what?'

'Oh, don't worry, we'd think of something,' Janice replied, eyes and teeth glittering.

The three of them all laughed loudly and hysterically. It was a bit alarming but the bell for lessons went at that point so nothing further was said.

'What do you think they're planning?' I asked Hazel and Leonie, another girl I liked.

'I don't know but you need to be very careful. They're really poisonous!'

'I know they're nasty,' I said. 'But do you really think they'll try to get me into trouble?'

There was a moment of silence and I noticed Leonie and Hazel exchanging meaningful looks.

'Yes, they *really* will,' answered Hazel with a sigh. 'They've done it before.'

'To you?' I asked.

'Yes, they did do it to me. But that wasn't particularly awful. They just told Miss McKenzie that I'd stolen money from them. They couldn't prove anything so I just had a big talk with Miss McKenzie and I made sure I told her what they were really like!'

'What we were thinking of, though,' Leonie continued the story, 'was what they did to a girl called Cheryl.'

'I'm not going to like this, am I?'

'No, it was horrible. They didn't like her. There was a reason. It was something to do with an argument between Cheryl's mum and Janice's mum. Anyway, they kept on making nasty comments to her or about her – about her clothes, her hair, her shoes, her face, her family – everything you could think of. Cheryl was a quiet girl and she didn't usually say anything back. Then one day they were making fun of her sister. We didn't know it at the time but her sister's disabled. Cheryl went mad. She screamed and shouted at them, then she rushed off to Mrs Doherty and told her everything the three of them had been doing. They were all excluded from school for a week and their mums were called up.'

'Serves them right,' I said, enjoying the thought of them squirming.

'Yes, but it didn't end there!' said Hazel.

'Go on, tell me what they did,' I urged.

'Well,' said Leonie, 'they did stop the nasty comments but they spent a long time whispering and plotting. After a while, we found out what they were up to. They stole several bus passes and purses and little things like hair slides and pens. Everyone in the class was getting upset at having their stuff stolen.'

'Most of us thought it was them, but we didn't have any proof,' added Hazel.

'Anyway, one morning Cheryl had her purse stolen with her locker key in it. Then, at afternoon registration Mrs Doherty came in looking incredibly angry. We were all silent. She talked to us about theft and keeping our belongings safe. Then she asked Cheryl to go out of the room with her.'

Hazel excitedly continued the story. 'We didn't know what was happening. Miss McKenzie kept us in the room in silence for ages – until Mrs Doherty popped her head round the door and said we could go. The only people who seemed to know what was happening were those three.'

'And they weren't saying anything,' put in Leonie. 'They were just smirking.'

'Anyway,' said Hazel, 'we didn't see Cheryl again

that day so in the evening I phoned her up. She was in a terrible state. Mrs Doherty had asked her to open her locker with the key that had been found. When she did, she found it was full of all the things that had been stolen – purses, pens, money, bus passes. Cheryl had told Mrs Doherty that she'd lost her purse and key that morning and someone else must have done this. But Mrs D. said there was a lot of evidence against her – and there were some girls who claimed to have seen her stealing.'

'Oh no! Did they really do that? I can't believe anyone could be that mean,' I said, horrified.

'That's why you must be very careful of those three!'

'But surely the rest of you said something.'

'Well, of course we did. Lots of us, including me and Leonie,' said Hazel, 'went to Miss McKenzie and Mrs Doherty to explain what we thought had really happened.'

'Well, why didn't they believe you?'

'Miss McKenzie did. I think she knows exactly what they're like. But Mrs Doherty said we had no real evidence except our dislike of those three and their dislike of Cheryl. Whereas, the items had been found in her locker.'

'But that's ridiculous. We all open our lockers in front of each other all the time. No one could ever hide all those things there without other people seeing them!'

'That's what we said to Mrs Doherty, but she said they were cleverly hidden in a bag at the back,' explained Hazel.

'But what happened to Cheryl?'

'Her mum was furious. Cheryl said there'd been big rows between her family and Janice's family. There was some kind of fight and the police were called. Anyway, Cheryl's mum wouldn't let her come back to the school.'

'So, really, those three won, didn't they?' I said.

'Yes. That's why you've got to be careful,' said Leonie earnestly.

'I reckon one day Cheryl will get her own back. Remember she said she and her mum were going to watch Janice until they caught her doing something they could get her into trouble for!'

'Well, I hope they do,' I said.

So you see, life at school is a bit hairy at times, but the Trio are really the only problem. Most of my teachers are very nice and I like the other girls in my class. I'm having ICT classes in the school's new computer room – just opened this term. It gives me a chance to find out what else I can do on the computer. I visited your website on the Net yesterday. You know, it's not half as good as Red Star's. I think you need to have another look, and improve it a bit. You also need a chatline – other bands have them!

Sorry, I shouldn't tell you what to do. I'm learning to do some simple programming now – I think I could really get into this sort of thing. It's incredibly simple once you know what to do.

Actually, there's been quite some excitement here at school. A new maths teacher has arrived called Mr Simms. Unfortunately, I don't have him for maths. I'm sure the girls who do can't get much work done. You see he looks just like Will Smith. I don't know if he's as jokey as Will Smith. He always looks very serious when I see him in the corridor or assembly. But I have seen him smiling – once – and he is certainly gorgeous. He walks around the school followed by little groups of gawping girls. Every time he's seen with a female member of staff, there's endless discussion about what their relationship is. It must be awful being such a good-looking man in a girls' school. Anyway, Mr Simms has had an amazing impact on maths at our school. You see, we're set in maths according to how good we are. I'm in the second set – which I was really pleased about. But Mr Simms teaches the top set in our year, so suddenly everyone in our group is working ridiculously hard. We have tests every half-term and can be moved up or down depending on the results, so, of course, everyone in our group is dying to get themselves moved up at half-term. Our teacher Miss Smythe is quite old – and she hasn't quite worked out what's happening. She just sits there beaming and saying, 'This is the keenest maths group I've taught for years. Splendid. Splendid.' *Splendid* is her favourite word. She says it every time someone asks her for yet another piece of extra homework or some help with a tricky problem. I'm no different to anyone else. I like Miss Smythe, she's a sweet old thing, but I think maths might be that much more exciting with the Will Smith looka-like. I'll keep you informed about the maths situation.

You're probably wondering why I haven't men-tioned home. It's because things have been quite quiet. Mum's been going down to the Job Centre every day to try and get some work. Last week, she had an interview at a bakery and got the job. She started today. She was really nervous. I made sure she was up on time and made her some breakfast. She said she needed a drink to steady her nerves but I'd hidden it all away the night before so she couldn't. Jake and I walked to the bakery with her this morning and took her in to make sure she got there. I just hope it lasts!

Well, I'm hoping you're going to be on *Top of the Pops* this week.

Bye for now.
Shelley

Don't let the
bullies win, Shelley.
Hang on in there.

Love
Ziggy

Shelley Wright
16 Waterstone House
London SE6

HUNGRY

Big macs, little macs,
Sausages, sweets,
Cream cakes, chocolate bars,
on screen, on walls, on magazines,
and I'm so hungry, so hungry

October 15

Dear Ziggy,

I was so excited when I got your card. I always hoped that you read my letters but I secretly suspected that a secretary just looks at the name and address and sends the cards. Now, at least I know someone reads them. I hope it's you – but of course I know you're really busy. I saw you on TOTP. You got to Number One! I hope the European tour goes well.

As usual, for me, things have gone from bad to worse or at least to a different kind of bad. Mum really enjoyed her first week at the bakery. She stayed sober, chatted to us in the evenings and brought us some really nice things for tea every day – because

41

they have to get rid of the left-over stock. Jake and I were really pleased.

On Thursday night, she promised that on the way home from work on Friday (pay day) she'd stop and get a video and some fish and chips. I was a bit worried about this (the fish and chip shop is next to the pub) so I suggested Jake and I came to meet her from work. She got really angry.

'Just stop this, Shelley,' she screamed. 'You're so suspicious. You don't have any faith in me. You think I'll drink it all away, don't you? Well, I won't. I just can't cope with your suspicion!'

So on Friday night Jake and I sat and watched television, waiting for her to come home. She finishes work at 5.30 so she should have been back by 6.00–6.30 at the latest. At 7 o'clock I went to see what was in the kitchen. We were both hungry. As usual, there was very little, but I managed to make us quite a nice supper – some tomato soup and toast (dry, no margarine left) followed by sardines on toast, followed by two not very fresh doughnuts. It wasn't *nouvelle cuisine* but it filled our stomachs. And I forgot to worry about things for a while because you and the band were live on TOTP and I managed to video it so I can watch you again whenever I like.

Well, as you can imagine, we didn't see Mum at all that evening. And she wasn't there when we woke up on Saturday. I wasn't too concerned – she was probably at Eileen's, but I didn't know how Jake and I were going to survive the weekend. We ate the rest of the bread and shared the last egg for breakfast. I was thinking of phoning Nan to tell her there was no food and no money when the phone rang. It wasn't Nan. It was Auntie Zandra, my dad's sister.

'Shelley, my darling, how are you?'

'OK, thanks,' I replied.

'Listen, darling. Fluff and I are having a little party today. It's our anniversary. Nothin' formal. Just a few friends and family coming round for a bit of lunch. You're not doing anything important are you?'

'No, nothing at all,' I answered.

'What about your mum?' she asked.

'Mum's out at the moment. She's started a new job.'

'A job! That's great! Now, you and Jake get round here about 1 o'clock. All right?'

'We'll be there. That's just great!' I answered, feeling as if my prayers had been answered. Auntie Zandra's 'bit of lunch' was usually a table groaning under the weight of bowls of rice, goat curry, jerk pork, chicken pieces, tiny patties, fruit salad, and lots of drinks. We'd be able to eat enough there to keep us going for the weekend. And she always said when we left that there was much too much left over and gave us a box of goodies.

Jake was really pleased. He is very fond of Auntie Zandra's little boy, Marlon, who is only two. Fluff is Zandra's new partner. His real name is Dr Aderogbe Oduyami. He's a very intense man who teaches incredibly complicated scientific things in the physics department at one of the London University Colleges. Everyone calls him Fluff – I've never discovered why.

Anyway, we spent the morning making an anniversary card on the computer. Then we left a note for Mum and set off. It was a long way and we had to walk – there wasn't any cash in the house for a bus or train. I hoped Dad might give us a lift back. We had a great time. They live in a huge old flat. It's quite different to the homes of most people I know, because it's full of African things. You see, Fluff's Nigerian and Zandra runs an Afro-Caribbean book and craft shop, so the flat's full of brightly printed cloth, carvings, screens, mats, pots and lots of photos of beautiful places in Africa. I love it. It's so cheerful and interesting.

We had a great time. We played with Marlon, saw Dad and Marilyn, let Nanny (Dad's mum) make a fuss of us and ate everything we could lay our hands on. When we saw the food Jake looked just like the little boy in the video you made for *Hunger*. You know, the one who's looking through the window into the restaurant with big round eyes and gaping mouth. By the time we left we were both feeling fat and full. And, just as I'd hoped, Zandra insisted on us taking a box of goodies with us.

Dad dropped us home. Mum was waiting for us in the living room.

'Did you have a good time?' she asked nicely.

'It was great,' said Jake. 'Marlon's grown since we last saw him. I played Action Man with him. He really liked it.' Jake was smiling broadly. It's not often he does that. And it's not often he says this much all in one go. Mum looked at him in a funny way.

'I'm glad you've enjoyed yourself, Jake. How about you, Shelley?'

I was a bit alarmed. Mum doesn't usually go in for these quiet calm questions. It was unfamiliar territory. I trod carefully.

'It was great. We made a card on the PC for

Zandra and Fluff's anniversary. They really liked it.'

'Did Zandra produce one of her huge spreads of food?' she asked. The same steady tone.

'Yeah. Lots of food. And as usual she made us bring some home with us. I'll put it in the kitchen.'

I moved quickly into the kitchen and pushed Jake towards the bedroom. Something strange was going on with Mum. When I opened the fridge to put the food away, there was already some milk, margarine, eggs, cheese and a chicken in it. Mum must have had some money left over from her wage packet. She appeared at the kitchen door and stared at me.

'You see. I can provide for my children. You don't have to go begging to your dad's family!' she snarled.

'Mum, we didn't go begging. Zandra phoned up and invited us this morning. It was a party. You were invited too but you weren't here!'

'Don't rub it in. I know I'm a hopeless mother. I suppose you told them that!'

'Of course not. We told them you were working in your new job.'

'Did you really?' she seemed surprised.

I went over to her and put my arms round her waist. She was soft and cuddly.

'Mum, why won't you ever believe me when I tell

you. We don't criticise you. Not to each other, not to friends, not to family.'

'I bet you tell your friends I drink too much.'

'Of course I don't. The only thing I've said to my friends is that you've got a new job.'

I could see her anger was breaking down.

'I will try and keep this job, Shelley. I really will. I want to be a good mum to you and Jake. I do really!'

'You are a good mum,' I said, and gave her a kiss. 'Now go and see how clever Jake is on the computer and I'll make a cup of tea.'

She went, and the rest of the weekend passed quite quietly. It was Monday evening when she slipped back into her old ways. She didn't come home after work. Jake and I ate the cold chicken and the remains of Zandra's feast. I was worried that if Mum was drinking all night she wouldn't get to work in the morning and she'd lose another job. She came home about 2.00 a.m. She fell through the door. I didn't get out of bed. I knew she'd accuse me of spying on her again. I heard things being knocked over and some retching. Fortunately, it was in the bathroom. Then peace. At least she was home safely.

It was really, really hard waking her up for work. She shouted and screamed and swore at us. I don't know how we did it, but we got her up, dressed, and walked her to the bakery. She was very pale, but at least she was there.

Since then, things have gone on very much like this. She's been going to the bookie's at lunchtime to bet on the horses and then going to the pub after work to spend her winnings or drown her sorrows. The only time we really see her is in the mornings when we face the daily battle of getting her up and into work.

So that's how my life has looked over the last two weeks. School's been quiet.

Hope this gets to you on tour.
Love,
Shelley

Thinking of you,
Shelley.

Love
Ziggy

Shelley Wright
16 Waterstone House
London SE6
Angleterre

SO COLD

You're so cold
Your love used to feel big as a mountain
No more mountain
Your love used to feel warm
As summer sun
No more summer
So cold, so cold

November 1

Dear Ziggy,

Thanks for the card. I saw you on TV – in Paris! And, of course, there were lots of reports about the girls who streaked at the airport when you arrived. Do you get a lot of that kind of thing?

I'll tell you about school first. This is both good and bad news. The strange thing is that the Trio have been suspiciously quiet. I know they're up to something. The rest of us are trying to work out what – but no success so far. Lessons are going just fine. As you can imagine I've been working really hard towards that half-term maths test. We took it the day before half-term and I get the results tomorrow. Fingers crossed I'll get into Mr Gorgeous's maths set.

Actually a couple of unusual things have happened at school. First, we had a really funny lesson. It was Personal and Social Education. We've been learning about relationships and sex and that sort of thing this term. Miss McKenzie gets a bit embarrassed sometimes and girls like Janice purposely ask embarrassing questions just to make her uncomfortable. Anyway, this lesson she brought in a big box and announced that she was going to show us some contraceptives.

So she delves into the box and brings out pills and strange items called diaphragms and coils and caps and baggy things called female condoms. Everyone oohs and ahs and says, 'I'm not going to put one of those anywhere near me!'

Then she announces that everyone is going to be given a condom and we're all going to learn how to put them on. Everyone began to laugh hysterically.

'Where are we going to put them?' someone said.

'Miss, it's the boys not us that wear those. I think you've got it a bit wrong, Miss,' said someone else.

'This is where we are going to put them,' said Miss McKenzie, delving into her box to bring out a carrot.

More hysteria.

'Now girls. These carrots were carefully chosen by Mrs Doherty to resemble the male organ. And there's one between two.'

'You said we'd have one each,' said Olivia.

'I said you'd have a condom each but only one carrot between two! Leonie, you give out one carrot between two. Shelley, could you give everyone a condom, please.'

I couldn't imagine there'd ever be another situation in my life where someone said that to me.

We sat with our carrots and our condoms while Miss McKenzie showed us how and told us when to put condoms on. We practised. It was the funniest, silliest, noisiest lesson we've ever had. When the bell went, Miss McKenzie counted all the condoms back into a bag and replaced the carrots.

'You're not going to eat those are you, Miss?' she was asked.

'I'm going to peel them, slice them, dice them, boil them and serve them in butter!' she answered, grinning wickedly.

'Ouch,' I thought, remembering what the carrots had represented a few minutes before.

Oh dear. I hope you aren't offended by my condom

story. No, I'm sure you won't be.

Two things were worrying me that week. First, Leonie and Hazel kept asking me round to their houses after school and they were arranging to meet during the half-term break and wanted me to come. I had two problems with this. If I go to their homes I really ought to invite them to mine – that's the first problem. Will Mum be there? Will she be drunk? Will one of her horrible friends be there? Will there be any food? I think I'm going to have to fill them in on some of the details before I dare invite them.

The other problem is Jake. I meet him every day from school. I'm not sure he'd get home safely if I didn't, and I am sure he'd be really frightened at the flat on his own. Even if Mum did come straight home from work, and that's unlikely, he'd be on his own for a while. And how could I go out at half-term and leave him on his own? He'd hate it. So, you see my problem. It's a shame. There's a couple of after-school clubs at school I'd really like to join, too. (No, not the maths club with Mr Simms. There were hundreds of people turning up for that – even Janice and Olivia and Charlene. They all had a real shock this week when Miss Smythe walked in to take the club instead of Mr Simms!) No, I meant the computer club and the drama group. Oh well, there'll be time later when Jake's older and more confident.

At least one of my problems was solved. Nan came round and took us to McDonald's for tea. When we told her it was half-term the following week, she told us we must come for lunch with her every day and we could stay for tea if we liked. I was really pleased. It meant we'd get some lunch and I'd be able to meet my friends without abandoning Jake. As things turned out, it was just as well she made the offer. On the Monday of half-term the gas was turned off because Mum hadn't paid the bill. We've got gas central heating so it was freezing cold. We had a little electric heater in the living room but nothing anywhere else. Mum said she couldn't get the gas turned back on until pay day on Friday, so we've been wearing lots of clothes. Apart from the cold, half-term was OK. Jake and I spent a lot of time in the library and had some really good dinners at Nan's. I managed to get some money from Dad to go out with Leonie and Hazel. It was great. We went shopping and then to the cinema. We were laughing all day and I had enough money left to take Jake to the cinema the following day.

The only real problems were the cold and Mum. We managed to get her to work on time but she was still spending most evenings drinking. One evening we stayed at Nan's quite late to watch a James Bond film. She insisted on bringing us home and came in with us. It was freezing cold and Mum was asleep on the settee surrounded by bottles. Nan went berserk.

'Wake up, Liz! What the hell do you think you're doing? Come on, clear this mess up!'

'Leave me alone, Mum,' said my mum.

'No I won't. You've got two children here and what kind of welcome do you give them. It's cold, it's dirty, and their mum's in a drunken stupor!'

'Just leave it, Mum.'

'No, I will not! Shelley, go and make your mother some strong coffee. Jakey darling, get yourself ready for bed and we'll make you a hot-water bottle. Why is it so cold in here, Liz?'

'The heating's gone wrong,' lied my mum as I went into the kitchen.

I could hear them rowing for some time. Finally, Nan came and hugged me, then left. When I took Mum her cup of tea (there wasn't any coffee) she stared at me.

'Why did you invite her back here?' She spoke in that same cold, strained voice I'd noticed before.

'I didn't. She just insisted on seeing us to the door.'

'Well, why didn't you see her off at the door?' she persisted.

'I tried. I said goodbye and stood at the door but she just pushed past me. You know she's not easy to stop if she's decided to do something.'

'Did you tell her about the heating?' she asked suspiciously.

'Of course I didn't! You heard her. She asked why it was so cold.'

'I suppose you'd prefer to go and live with her. She'd be a better mother to you than me.'

'No she wouldn't.'

'But at least her house is warm!'

'So will ours be when you pay the bill on Friday, Mum.'

'I suppose so.'

She just sat there. Usually, at this stage in conversations like this, she'd start to cry and hug me and apologise for her faults. But she didn't. She just sat motionless and emotionless. No tears. No hugs. No apologies. Just a cold, empty silence. And her face set in an expression of stony misery.

It frightened me, Ziggy. It frightened me much more than her drinking, screaming and crying. I've learnt how to deal with those. I'm at a loss now. I don't know how to deal with her in this state.

Oh dear. I seem to be ending this letter on a depressed note. Don't worry. I'll play *Dreams*. It always makes me optimistic.

Love,
Shelley

Hang on in there,
Shelley.
Keep dreaming.

Love Ziggy

Shelley Wright
16 Waterstone House
London SE6

HURT

You really know how to hurt,
You twist the knife
In my heart
You bite the layer of
Chocolate confidence
That covers my soft centre

November 15

Dear Ziggy,
Thanks for your card. It arrived on a bad day and everything improved. But not for long. In my last letter I told you how strangely my mum was behaving – all cold and distant. Well, it got worse. The week after half-term, Jake and I got home one afternoon and found her at home crying. She'd gone to the bookie's at lunchtime the day before and won a bit of money. So she'd gone to the pub to celebrate and didn't get back to work in the afternoon. Apparently it wasn't the first time it had happened, because when she got into the bakery the next morning the manager

57

told her she was fired.

I was really disappointed but I tried to be cheerful. I said, 'Never mind, I'm sure you can get another job.'

'Don't be stupid, Shelley,' she said. 'You know that's unlikely.'

'You got this one. What's to stop you getting another?' I replied.

'Don't be so patronising. I'm sick of you treating me like a kid. You're the kid here, not me!'

'All right, all right, I'm sorry,' I said, trying to keep the peace and noticing Jake scuttling to the bedroom, his hands over his ears. 'I was just trying to cheer you up.'

'Well, don't bother. You only make me mad. Just don't say anything.'

'OK,' I agreed.

A few minutes later she went out. I thought that would be the last we'd see of her all evening so I started to make some scrambled egg for our tea. We were sitting eating it and watching *Neighbours* when she came back. She'd bought some fish and chips for us all for tea. She came in smiling, then took one look at us eating our scrambled egg and the smile froze. So did we.

'I see you've already got something to eat,' she said in a very stiff voice.

'Not much,' I said. 'It's just a bit of scrambled egg. We didn't know you'd gone to buy chips.'

'I'd really like some chips, Mum,' said Jake.

She stood and stared at us for a while. Then she just dropped the chips and her purse on the floor.

'I can't do anything right, can I?' she said miserably. 'Even when I try to look after you and give you treats, something goes wrong. Something always goes wrong!'

'Nothing's gone wrong, Mum. Let's eat the chips.'

I put my plate down and went to pick them up.

'Leave them alone!' she shouted. I stood still. 'Just leave them alone. If you're going to eat them, *I'll* pick them up and *I'll* serve them and we'll sit at the table to eat them!'

I groaned inwardly. The table was strewn with my history work. I'd been doing research on women munition workers in the First World War and I was in the middle of putting it all together to give in at the end of the week.

'Couldn't we sit by the telly?' I asked very gently.

'No! We're going to be a proper family having proper tea round a proper table! Clear it!'

'But—' I started.

It was a mistake.

'No buts,' she said, and slapped me across my face. I was shocked. I stood still, a bit dazed, my cheek stinging.

'Clear that rubbish off!' she shouted.

'It's not rubbish! It's my history project!' I argued.

'I don't care what it is. Get rid of it!'

I've always tried to keep calm and patient with Mum but suddenly it was all too much. Every day I looked after Jake and myself while she drank, and now, on the one day she brings home some tea, she makes this fuss. I didn't say anything but I didn't move to clear it away either.

There was a moment of silence when we glared at each other. Then she moved, incredibly quickly, to the table and, picking up a sheaf of papers, she tore the whole wad in two.

'Noooo!' I screamed, and rushed to save my work. I grabbed what I could as she swept it onto the floor. I sat on the floor looking at the torn pieces: my best writing; some work done on the computer; some drawings and graphs. All torn. I burst into angry tears.

'How could you do that? I've spent ages doing this!'

'Well, you should have moved it when I told you to!' she answered.

'You just don't care at all, do you?' I shouted.

To my surprise, Jake came over and sat on the floor beside me. It was a surprise because he usually scuttles away or keeps quiet during any arguments.

'Mum,' he said in a very quiet, tiny voice. 'You shouldn't have done that. Shelley's worked really—'

He didn't manage to finish the sentence.

Mum hit him across the side of his head. 'You can shut up!' she screamed.

I put my arms round Jake. He was crying and shaking. I thought she was going to hit one or both of us again but she stepped back.

'You don't really need me, do you?' she said in a sneering kind of way. 'Well, you've got your way. I'll leave you to it. Enjoy your chips!'

And she left. Once we'd cleared up and calmed down we both discovered we were *really* hungry and strangely we did enjoy the chips! I managed to rescue some but not all of my history work, but we didn't see Mum again for two days.

Well, that was my low point. Since that day there's been a kind of unnatural calm. We've all been moving round each other very carefully. So life at home has been a bit strained.

School's had its good and its bad moments. You remember everyone was desperately trying to do well in the maths test so they could be in the top group with Mr Gorgeous. Well, I managed it. So did my friend Leonie. We were pretty amazed! Anyway, maths lessons have taken on a whole new complexion.

Some of the group are simply keen on maths and they don't appear to take any notice of Mr Simms except to listen to directions and ask questions. The rest of us spend time gazing, taking in his hair (very close cut); his skin (smooth); his neat ears; his quick, brilliant smile; his broad shoulders; his expensive-looking shirts and silk ties; his suits – one dark green, one chocolate brown (that's my favourite) and one black; his shoes – one pair black suede, one pair brown leather. But most of all, it's the way he moves – he has expressive, constantly moving hands with long fingers, neatly cut nails and a ring on one finger.

Lots of the girls ask questions so he'll come over to their desks. Yesterday, a girl called Olamide purposely dropped her pencil when he was nearby. She was hoping to get a closer look at his bum!

We were all a bit disappointed when he turned to help someone else and ignored the pencil. I am of course continuing to work hard, trying to impress Mr Simms or at least make sure I stay in his group.

Meanwhile, the Trio have yet again been making life difficult for everyone. Last Tuesday they were messing about at dinner time and got *Coke* all over the new carpet in the classroom. At registration we were all hoping Miss McKenzie wouldn't notice. Of course she did. She was livid.

'I want to know exactly what that mess is on the carpet,' she announced.

There was silence. I noticed Janice giving warning signs to some of the class.

'Not very impressive,' said Miss McKenzie. 'Now, I want to know who is responsible. Who was it?'

An even longer embarrassing silence.

'Then I'll tell you what I'll do,' said Miss McKenzie. 'I'll give everyone a little piece of paper and on it you can each write the name of the girl or girls who were responsible.'

There was a groan.

'OK. I know this is annoying for you,' she countered, 'but I'm sure most of you are as angry as I am about the cowardice we're seeing here. It would have been no big deal if someone had simply told me there'd been an accident but now it's a different matter. I don't like cowardice like this. So I *will* find out who did it!'

I had no hesitation in writing down the names of the lovely Trio on my bit of paper. I wanted them punished and humiliated. Miss McKenzie took everyone's piece of paper and, glaring at us all in disgust, told us to leave.

There were mutterings and gossip throughout the afternoon. Then Miss McKenzie came into our ICT lesson just as the bell was going. We all had to sit in silence again. 'I've come to give you the result of my little survey,' she said brightly. 'I knew you'd have sleepless nights if you didn't know! Here it is: one person named Sarah. (There was a gasp, a giggle, and a huge blush from Sarah.) I'm discounting that one. Four people wrote "I don't know". One smart alec wrote "Mr Bean". I'm discounting him too. Three people wrote Shelley and Hazel. Those of you who are paying attention may be able to work out that there are still seventeen votes unaccounted for. All seventeen of them name the same three girls: Janice, Charlene and Olivia. So, my guess – and I have seventeen witnesses – is that our cowardly culprits are Janice, Charlene and Olivia. You three stay behind. The rest of you can go.'

And we went. We heard the following day – unendingly – that they'd had to shampoo the carpet and clean graffiti off the toilet walls. I was really pleased they'd got into trouble, but I sensed danger in the air. They felt humiliated and for some reason Hazel and Leonie and I got the blame. The Trio also seemed to think the whole class had turned against them. They couldn't really accept that they had only themselves to blame for their own unpopularity.

I'll keep you informed on their next moves.

Love,
Shelley

Hang on in there,
Shelley.

Love
Ziggy

Shelley Wright
16 Waterstone House
London SE6

PUSHING CLOUDS AWAY

Just the smallest gleam,
The smallest speck of light
And I'm pushin' pushin' pushin'
Pushin' the clouds away

December 1

Dear Ziggy,

Thanks for your card and the little photo that came with it. I feel so lucky that you take the time to send me replies. You'll be pleased to know that I have been able to push some clouds away!

I've joined the computer club at school, which I've been wanting to do all term. Jake's school has started an after-hours club so he stays there on Tuesday afternoons and I pick him up later. He's quite happy – he gets to use the computers there and I'm learning to make databases and create a website. Exciting stuff. There's another interesting development at school – this time it doesn't concern the Trio. Yesterday, our maths lesson began quite normally with the register and everyone carefully studying Mr Simms. Then we had to get our books out to write the date and title – he was going to start a new topic. I was getting out my book when I realised everyone was giggling. Mr Simms was at the board looking at the class in surprise.

'Calm down, girls,' he said. 'I didn't think you found solving equations that exciting!'

I couldn't see why people were laughing. Then he turned round to write the title on the board and everyone, including me, burst out laughing. There on his back someone had stuck a piece of paper with the neatly typed (in big print) words:

> Underneath this
> immaculate suit
> I'm wearing . . .
> nothing at all!

He turned round again.

'What *is* the matter?' he asked, getting annoyed.

No one said anything.

'Come on. Something's amusing you!' he urged.

So one of the girls said, 'Sir, someone's put something on your back,' and we watched him reach round for it, then read it. There was silence. He looked up at us all very seriously. I thought, 'Oh no he's going to be livid.' Then he burst out laughing.

'I think I need to make a couple of things clear,' he announced. 'First, it's not true. Second, I'm not letting anyone check. Third, I don't approve of this – but it's quite amusing. Lastly – we have work to do!'

It cheered me up no end because I'd just had a pretty nasty encounter with the Trio. I just happened to go into the toilets by the gym during break time. They were in there smoking with a few others.

'Well, look who it is,' Janice said when I went in.

I wanted to run back out again but I didn't want to appear intimidated.

'It's our friend or rather Miss McKenzie's friend! Come to spy, have you?' asked Olivia.

I ignored them and went over to wash the mud off my hands.

'Oh, she won't reply!' Janice went on. 'You don't think she wants to talk to the likes of us, do you?'

They all made a stupid 'Oo oo' noise and I continued to ignore them.

'I suppose you'll run straight to Miss to tell her what we're doing!' Olivia went on.

I turned round to her. 'I won't have to tell her, she'll be able to smell the smoke on you!' I said.

'And on you!' laughed Janice, coming right up to

me and blowing smoke in my face.

'That's revolting!' I said.

'Suits you then, doesn't it?' she answered, laughing and sneering.

They all joined in. It was nightmarish. I wanted to run out but I walked – I was determined they wouldn't see me scared! I really did want to tell Miss McKenzie and get them into trouble but of course I didn't.

They're getting worse. Constantly whispering and giggling and making comments. Last week it was my trainers when we were changing for PE.

'Where did you get your trainers, Shelley?' Janice called out loudly. Of course everyone looked at them. I ignored her.

'She doesn't want to tell you. Designer shops get so crowded if too many people go there!' mocked Olivia.

'Since when was Oxfam a designer shop?' replied Janice.

Some of the others laughed. I'm sure I blushed. Leonie said, 'Take no notice.'

But of course it was embarrassing.

Then, today, Janice simply stuck her foot out as I was passing her and I tripped over. I didn't hurt myself but I was angry.

'Why did you do that, Janice?' I said.

'Do what?' she asked, looking at me all surprised.

'Trip me up, of course!' I yelled.

'Why on earth would I do that?' she continued slowly.

'Your usual spitefulness, I expect!' I said.

'Oh dear. We're a bit uptight today, aren't we?' said her sidekick, Olivia.

'Only when I'm tripped up!' I said.

'Poor thing,' Janice took up the theme. 'She probably didn't sleep well!'

'Well, it must be cold in a cardboard box in this weather!' added Charlene, and they all burst into hysterical laughter. I just stormed off. It's difficult to know what to do. I just know that one of these days I'm going to get so mad, I'll probably thump one of them. And it's bound to be me that lands in trouble for it.

Sometimes I imagine what it must be like to have the kind of mum you could discuss things like that with. It must be nice. I can't. She'd just get wound up and go to the school drunk and make a fool of herself and embarrass me. So I tell her everything's fine. I have told Dad. He says I should tell Miss McKenzie. But I haven't. I think they'll be even worse if I do.

Since she lost her job Mum's been impossible. She's either at her friend's or at the pub. When she's at home she's usually asleep. I don't mind that. The problem is that she wakes up in the middle of the night and disturbs us. Usually, she just comes in saying she's checking her little ones are asleep. Of course she falls over, swears, falls again, then flops onto the bed – by which time I'm wide awake. Then she witters on about her lovely babies or starts crying and saying she's sorry. It usually ends with her falling asleep on my bed so I have to go and sleep on the settee. Last night was worse than usual. She was up and about when we got home and made us some tea. It was nice. She can cook really well. Then Jake watched television and I did my homework.

It was all quite peaceful. She even made us both some hot chocolate before bed. That was when everything went wrong. Jake accidentally knocked his chocolate over. It went on his legs and he screamed because it burnt him. She just went mad. Instead of checking he was OK, she just shouted at him.

'Stop screaming, you idiot,' she yelled.

He didn't stop.

'Stop it, stop it!' she went on. 'You're so bloody clumsy. You stupid child! There's something the matter with you. You're so silent. You stare at me all the time. Then you throw the drink all over the place. You wouldn't have done that if your precious sister had made it for you would you?'

Jake was still crying and trying to pull his pyjama trousers off.

'Leave him, Mum,' I said.

'There you go again!' she screamed at me. 'Telling me what to do! You just stay out of this, Shelley. For God's sake, Jake, stop that screaming and crying!'

He didn't stop. He was too shocked and upset.

'Stop it, stop it!' she yelled.

Then, she suddenly grabbed him and shook him really hard. He was frightened and screamed even more.

'Stop!' she yelled again and smacked him across his face. He crumpled onto the floor just as I got to him.

'Leave him alone, Mum, *please*!' I said.

She raised her hand to hit me as well. I put my hand up to shield my head, but the blow never fell. She stood staring at me, then sank onto the settee and started crying.

I took Jake to the bathroom and we put cold water on his burn and he calmed down. I read him a story and he was soon asleep. So was she. I just sank onto the floor with my head in my hands and cried. I really don't know what to do. I used to love Mum so much, but I hate her when I see her treat Jake like that.

What can I do? If I tell Dad or Nan or Zandra, they'll have a go at Mum. I can't tell anyone else in case they report it to Social Services. That can't happen. They might split me and Jake up. I'd die rather than let that happen.

Anyway, I think Mum's feeling guilty. When we got home today she'd cleaned up and baked a cake for us. We sat and had tea and cake. She asked us about school as if we were a perfectly normal family. Then she said she had to go and see her friend and we haven't seen her since. So it's been a calmer day today. What's more, Janice was away, so the other two were pretty quiet and pleasant, *and* I saw you being interviewed on *Give us Five* this afternoon.

So, today, I definitely pushed those clouds away.

Love,
Shelley

Keep pushing,
Shelley.

Love
Ziggy

Shelley Wright
16 Waterstone House
London SE6

WINTER BLUES

I'm gonna
Wrap it up,
Rap it up,
Wrap it all for you,
Rap it all for you,
To keep the winter blues away

December 15

Dear Ziggy,
The card arrived at just the right moment. I was feeling really depressed. Everyone at school had been making huge lists of people to send Christmas cards to and lists of people to buy presents for. I did it too and realised I was going to need loads of money. It's no good asking Mum for any at the moment. I phoned Dad and he was out. I phoned Nan and she was out. So Jake and I went round to Auntie Zandra's shop to ask her advice. She always seems wise and sensible. As we approached the shop I could see there was something different about it. Usually, it has very

bright window displays with yellow or orange back-grounds and lots of interesting things in. But the window looked brown and dull. Coming closer, we saw that the window was boarded up. We went inside. Auntie Zandra was there and gave us her usual big smile and hug. But then she burst into tears.

'What's the matter?' I asked.

'It's the window,' she said.

'What happened to it?' I asked.

'Some idiot threw a brick through it,' she told us.

'Do you know who?' I asked.

'Not exactly, but they left a calling card.' She showed me a little card. On one side it had a Union Jack and a Bulldog. On the other, it said, 'Why don't you move your filthy little shop to where it belongs – like Africa!'

'That's horrible!' I cried. 'What did the police say?'

'Not much. It happened in the night and they don't think there are likely to be any witnesses.'

'What about fingerprints and that sort of thing?' asked Jake who was keen on detective stories.

'The policeman says they're unlikely to find much evidence. You see, they didn't come in.'

'Well, I suppose it would have been much worse if they had,' I said, looking around. There were so many things in the shop they could have damaged: books, rugs, masks, posters, pots, carvings, tapes. That would have been a real disaster.

'Is someone coming to mend the window?' I asked.

'Yes. They're coming to fit one of those horrible metal grilles. I had it all measured up this morning. It's just so sad that I've got to do that!'

Jake and I helped her tidy up and she invited us to come over at the weekend to play with Marlon.

Well – as you can imagine we were still a bit upset when we got home. I was just warming some soup for tea when the doorbell went. It was our next-door neighbour. He's an old Polish man called Andresz who keeps a white cat and a black rat and talks to them all day. He had his rat (called Leopold) on his shoulder.

'That stupid postman. He delivered this to me instead of you. You're lucky Leopold didn't eat it. He was very interested!'

I stroked Leopold (who's very good natured) and thanked Andresz. He always gives the impression that he's a bad-tempered old bloke but in fact he's very kind to me and Jake.

I looked at the card. It was from you and immediately my gloomy mood lifted.

What's more, your card had a magical effect. Almost as soon as I read it Dad came round. When he saw Mum wasn't there he ordered a pizza.

'I wanted to talk to your mum about Christmas,' he told us.

'I don't think she's thought about it yet,' I told him.

'No, I don't suppose she has. I'll tell you my worry, Shelley. I'd like to have you two round over Christmas but Marilyn went to the clinic today and they think the baby might come early – which means over Christmas!'

'That would be great!' I said.

'Yes and no. I don't want to make arrangements and then have to change them all. So I've phoned up your nan and we made some plans. She'd like you all to go over there for dinner on Christmas Day and if you want you can stay overnight. See what your mum says about that. Then, on Boxing Day, I'll pick you up and we'll all go to Zandra's for the day. How does that sound?'

'It sounds great, Dad,' I said and gave him a hug. Jake agreed. Then I broached the delicate subject of money.

'There's just one little problem,' I started. Dad held his hand up.

'I know what you're thinking, Shelley. Your mum will make a fuss and tell us we're taking over her life. Don't worry. Your nan is going to sort it all out with her.'

'That's good, but it wasn't what I was thinking—'

'And the other problem is money!' Dad grinned. 'You see, angel, I think of everything. Here's enough money for you to buy cards and presents. You'll need a tree as well – the decorations are in a box some-where. I'll come over on Christmas Eve and we'll go shopping for some food and things. Take the enve-lope. Hide it. Don't tell your mum you've got it. She'll either take it or get into a rage about it. Now don't be extravagant, but make sure you get presents. I'll come and pick Jake up after school next Thursday and we'll go and do a bit of private shopping. OK, Jakey?'

Jake beamed. He loves the rare moments when he has Dad to himself.

Dad soon went off. He didn't want to be there when Mum got back in case there was some awful scene. So you see your card not only cheered me up but it was a good luck charm. My worries were all sorted out, and I've got enough to buy a little present for Hazel and Leonie. So I'm engaged in some serious planning now!

School's been a bit strange this week, we got into big trouble in art because Janice had stolen a whole pack of felt-tip pens. Of course, the teacher counted the packs at the end of the lesson. When one was missing she got us all looking for it. No luck. Then she told us to empty our bags. We did so and Miss Lemon (yes, that really is her name) checked them all. Still no luck. Then the pens turned up in a plant pot which was quite close to Janice. She pretended to be surprised. Miss Lemon wasn't too worried – she just wanted them back. On her way out Janice whispered to me, 'Don't cut your eye at me!'

'I wasn't!' I said. But she walked on with her mates. In the form room Olivia turned on me.

'Why were you cutting your eye at Janice, just now?'

'I wasn't. Janice imagined it,' I answered.

'Are you suggesting I'm stupid?' said Janice in a menacing way.

'No, but you might be mistaken,' I said.

'No. I don't make that kind of mistake,' she said, trying to sound the big tough woman.

I tried to ignore her. It was difficult. She came and planted herself right in front of me.

'I don't like people cutting their eye at me,' she

said, wagging her finger.

'I don't like people wagging their fingers at me,' I said, starting to get angry.

'I'm just warning you, Shelley High and Mighty. You do that again and I'll box you!'

I wanted to smash her in the face. But over her shoulder I saw Leonie mouthing 'Don't do it' at me, and Hazel frowning. So I took a deep breath, stepped back and smiled.

'Don't worry, Janice. I'll try not to look at you at all!' I walked away, keeping a steady pace. I really am trying not to let that girl get to me, Ziggy, but it's hard. I know I'm going to lash out one of these days!

Well, the Trio stayed away from me after that. And I soon forgot about Janice because something funny happened. The phantom placer-of-notes-on-teachers' backs struck again. This time it was in science. Our science teacher is a very stern middle-aged lady. She has grey hair cut short and severe, grey-rimmed glasses, and wears either a grey suit with a pleated skirt and white blouse or a navy suit with pleated skirt and pale blue blouse. That day it was the grey suit.

Miss Hemingway was sitting at her desk when we came in. She did the register and told us what we were going to do and we read some of the text book.

It was very boring. Then she explained something that wasn't in the book (it was about electrical current) and said she was going to put a flow diagram on the board which we must copy. Then of course it happened. She turned to write on the board and the class collapsed in wild laughter. The same neat typing. A similar message. This one said:

> Underneath this
> boring grey suit
> I'm wearing . . .
> very sexy red panties!

Miss Hemingway turned to us in astonishment, then anger.

'What on earth—?' she began, but someone shouted: 'On your back, Miss!' She twisted her arm round and pulled off the paper.

Miss Hemingway, unlike Mr Simms, was not amused. She stared at the paper. Then glared at us. We went silent.

'One of you, I presume?' she said, glaring all around at us.

'It couldn't have been, Miss,' said one very brave soul. 'You were at your desk when we came in and no one's been out of their seat!'

Miss Hemingway was about to shout at her but she stopped short.

'You're right, for once!' she said. 'And I sincerely hope none of you have had anything to do with this. I will make it my business to find the culprits!'

'I wouldn't like to be in their shoes when she does!' I whispered to Leonie.

'You have a comment, Shelley?' said Miss Hemingway, sharp as mustard.

'I just said, "I hope you do, Miss",' I said, trying to sound sincere.

That was the end of the matter. Back to electricity. But I couldn't help wondering what kind of underwear Miss Hemingway might wear.

Hope you have a great Christmas.
Love,
Shelley

Happy Christmas,
Shelley.

Ziggy

Shelley Wright
16 Waterstone House
London SE6

A BIT OF JOY

Hey girl, hey boy,
Stop,
Take time out,
Find a bit of joy

January 1

Dear Ziggy,
Happy New Year! I hope you had a great Christmas. I saw you on the Boxing Day *Chart of the Year Show*. You looked as if you were enjoying yourself and I loved that T-shirt!

It seems ages since my last letter. I can't believe it's only two weeks, such a lot has happened!

The end of term at school was fun. The day before term ended, we had what's called a 'Fun Day' when everyone has to think up some game or event to raise money for charity. Our class ran a disco in one of the gyms. It was quite good. Miss McKenzie had persuaded her brother to fix up some lighting and two of the girls did the DJing. We made lots of money –

everyone came in for a while to dance. The only problem, of course, was that there were no boys. But it beat geography lessons any day. One of the other classes had arranged a game where you throw wet sponges at the teachers. They came dressed in wet suits and cagoules and bath hats – but it was still great to watch them with water dripping down their faces.

The last day of term we had a big assembly with songs and readings. It was all going very smoothly, until the end. Then it was the Head's turn. She had been at the back of the stage. She came forward and read us a little poem. Then she began to congratulate everyone on their singing and reading. The readers were sitting, grinning, in a row behind her and she turned round to thank them. It was then we all saw it! The whole school. You can probably guess. Yes, there on the back of her smart red suit was a neatly typed note. I was sitting at the side near enough to see what it said:

> Underneath this smart
> red suit I'm wearing . . .
> black shiny leather!

First, there was a ripple of laughter, then everyone joined in. The whole school was laughing! Perplexed, the Head just stared at us for a moment. She went bright red and we all thought she was going to explode. Then, quick as a flash, the Deputy Head rushed up to her, pulled the note off her back and gave it to her. We were watching her every move. She read it, and paused. I wasn't sure how she was going to react. She stood still, staring at it. I saw the Deputy say something to her. Then she looked up and looked all around the hall. After a very tense moment, she smiled.

'I'll consider this to be Christmas high spirits,' she said. 'And I should probably point out that this is not true.'

Everyone started laughing again. I was really impressed. I think I'd have gone mad and made a fool of myself if I'd been her.

Then the holiday started. Mum had a job in a supermarket, just for the week before Christmas. She was doing really well – getting up early and going to the staff canteen, not the pub, at lunchtime. She brought home bits and pieces of food every day because they had to dispose of everything before the sell-by date. One night she brought home a whole tray of yogurts; the next, she brought home packs of turkey slices. So we had an unusual diet!

Jake and I went shopping on the first day of our holiday and bought lots of presents and wrapping paper. When we got home we quickly decorated the tree and put up some other decorations. Then we watched out for Mum arriving home from work. We turned off the lights in the living room and crouched down behind the tree. When she opened the door we flicked on the tree lights and jumped up. Mum was delighted. She lit some candles and we sat and ate mince pies and pork pies by candlelight, admiring our pretty tree.

The following day I went to do a bit more Christmas shopping with Nan and managed to tick off all the names on my present list. Christmas Eve was hectic. Jake and I got the house clean and tidy, then Dad took us to the supermarket and bought biscuits and drinks and cold meat and all sorts of little snacks and treats. When Mum came home we had a special Christmas Eve tea and watched all those comedy programmes they put on TV.

Unfortunately, Mum's friend Eileen called round and dragged her out 'for a quick Christmas drink', so we didn't see her again that night. I heard her come home, in the early hours and bounce off the walls on her way to bed.

Well, Christmas Day began early because Jake was so excited. We went into the kitchen and made lots of breakfast. Orange juice, cereal, coffee and toast. We tried to wake Mum up but it was hard. She murmured 'Happy Christmas' and went straight back to sleep. So we opened some of our presents. Dad had bought us a colour printer and some computer games. Jake had bought me a wind chime and some bath bubbles. I'd bought him an Action Man, which he was really pleased with. We played and watched the television. By 12 o'clock Mum still hadn't emerged so we went to wake her. We took her coffee and pulled her so she was sitting up. After that she stopped groaning and we gave her our presents – a pretty blouse and a little silver necklace. She was really pleased.

We all went off to Nan's and had a huge Christmas dinner and more presents. It was great. We did all the usual Christmas things – played silly games, pulled crackers, watched soppy films. After tea we had the best fun. Nan got a karaoke system for Christmas, so we all had a go. We sounded dreadful! You should have heard Mum's impression of Tina Turner singing *Simply the Best*. You know I was dreading Christmas but in fact it was fine. Boxing Day was all dancing and joking too – and no sign of the baby yet!

I knew it was too good to last. Two days after Christmas, Jake and I came home from the library to find the air thick with smoke, and bottles and cans and various people I'd never seen before all over the living room. I took Jake to our room. Mum followed me in.

'Don't look so disapproving, Madam,' she slurred, waving a bottle in one hand and a cigarette in the other.

'I was just surprised,' I lied.

'I wish you'd come and talk to my friends,' she continued.

'Jake and I want to play a game,' I said. 'Anyway, we don't know any of those people.'

'Oh, don't worry,' she said bitterly. 'I know. You look down on my friends. They aren't good enough. You'll be sociable and talk to Auntie Zandra's friends at her house but when I have a little party it's different. They're not worth speaking to.'

I didn't answer. I couldn't think of anything to say that wouldn't make things worse. She just stared at me, then at Jake.

'Come on, Jakey. You come and talk to Mummy's friends!' She grabbed his hand. Jake pulled away.

She stood swaying, looking from one to the other of us.

'You little bitch,' she spat. 'You've even turned my little boy against his mother!'

And with that she swayed out of the room and slammed the door. I gave Jake a hug and told him she'd forget about it straightaway and so should he. A couple of hours later we heard them all leaving. I spent ages cleaning up their mess.

The rest of the week continued like that. Mum was out most of the time. When she was home she was asleep or in a bad mood because she had a hangover.

Then yesterday, as it was New Year's Eve, Mum told us she was going to make us a really nice meal. She'd bought a chicken and was going to roast some potatoes, and she'd bought an apple pie and cream. The trouble was she went out 'for a newspaper' at lunchtime and by 6 o'clock she still wasn't back. Jake and I looked in a cookery book, then we put the chicken and potatoes in the oven and found some peas and carrots. We laid the table with a cloth and serviettes and candles. I don't know how the chicken ever cooked because I kept opening the oven door to check it.

Anyway, Mum did get home, at about 8 o'clock. We told her it was her New Year surprise and she burst into tears. She told me it was the best meal she'd ever had. (Surprisingly, it was quite edible.)

Everything was fine. Then it all turned sour. Jake and I were chucking cushions at each other and laughing like mad. Then Jake threw a cushion and it hit a little china vase of Mum's. The vase fell and smashed. Mum came rushing in from the kitchen. She was furious when she saw it broken.

'Who did that?' she shouted.

'I did,' said Jake in a tiny voice. 'I'm really sorry, Mum.'

'Don't give me *sorry*, you stupid, clumsy idiot!' She was shouting even louder. 'I've had that vase since I was ten and now you go and break it!'

'I'm sorry,' squeaked Jake in tears.

'Stop saying you're sorry. That's all you ever say. You're so bloody pathetic, Jake. You hardly say a word, then when you do, it's something weedy like "I'm sorry!" Just shut up!'

'I'm sor—' Jake began again but stopped when he realised what he was about to say. He started sobbing.

'Stop that noise! Stop snivelling!'

Jake tried, sniffing.

'Stop it! I can't bear that sniffing and snivelling. Stop it or I'll give you something to cry about!'

I could feel Jake trying to control his sobbing but he couldn't. Mum lunged forward and hit him around the head.

'Don't hurt him,' I shouted.

She looked at me, eyes blazing.

'Don't tell me what to do!' she screamed and came towards me, hand raised to hit me too. I stood up to face her and grabbed her raised arm by the wrist. She swore and took a swipe at me with the other hand. I grabbed that too. We stood in the middle of the room, me struggling to keep hold of her arms, Mum straining to free them so she could slap me. Then there was this strange moment of stillness. I suddenly realized I was as big and as strong as my mother. I was no longer a little child she could hit. I could now fight back. I think the same thing dawned on her, because she was totally still as she stared at me. It was quite a scary moment. I felt angry and frightened but also quite powerful. Whatever it was that happened in that moment it solved the immediate problem. Mum dropped her arms and stormed out – out of the room and out of the flat.

So, last year ended strangely. But today it's a new year, a new start. I'm sure your year will be filled with excitement and success. I'm hoping mine will be better than the last.

Love,
Shelley

Happy New Year, Shelley. I'm sure it'll be better than the last.

Love
Ziggy

Shelley Wright
16 Waterstone House
London SE6

REACHING OUT

Reaching out for
A new dawn
A new breath
A tiny form
Reaching out for life

January 15

Dear Ziggy,
It was great to get your card. Again, it arrived just when I needed a boost.

After I posted my last letter, Mum came home and I overheard her talking to Dad on the phone, complaining about how difficult life was and how awkward we were being. About half an hour later Dad arrived and we went off to his house.

Marilyn had made a really nice pie for us and we were enjoying our dinner. Dad was telling the most corny jokes and we were all trying to think of stupid knock-knock jokes.

'Knock, knock,' said Jake.

93

'Who's there?' we asked for the hundredth time.

'Putta.'

'Putta who?'

'Putta kettle on and we'll have a cup of tea.'

Well, we were all groaning at the awfulness of this when Marilyn gave a little cry. We all stared at her. She was clutching her belly.

'Oh, Ben!' she said. 'I think it's all starting.'

Dad leapt up and rushed over to her.

'What do you want me to do? Should we phone the hospital? Where's your bag? How soon?' he said, panicking.

'It's all right,' said Marilyn calmly. 'It's not going to be for a while. First, we've got to time the contractions!'

Jake and I were frightened. We wanted to help but didn't know what to do. Dad sat down with Marilyn and took off his watch.

'Is there anything I can do?' I asked.

There wasn't. So Jake and I cleared the table, washed up and made a cup of tea. Marilyn said that was the best idea I could possibly have had. Then she winced and clutched her huge tummy.

'Again!' she said.

'Eight minutes,' said Dad.

'OK,' said Marilyn. 'I need to phone the hospital *now*.'

She phoned, then went upstairs to finish packing her bag. Dad followed her around with the watch.

'Five minutes that time,' he said. 'Shouldn't we be getting to the hospital now?'

He was obviously frightened that Marilyn might not get there in time. She kept telling him not to worry. He phoned Auntie Zandra and arranged for her to meet us at the hospital so she could take care of us. We set off and since Dad was driving, I was given charge of the watch. I had to measure the time between contractions – which meant the time from one of Marilyn's shrieks to the next. The journey seemed to take ages. Marilyn was also beginning to get worried. Suddenly the time between shrieks went from four minutes to two. Marilyn was obviously in quite a lot of pain. Dad and Jake looked terrified.

Well, we got there. A nurse took Marilyn and Dad off. Jake and I sat in a little waiting room worrying. It was such a relief when Auntie Zandra, Fluff and little Marlon came in. Zandra always gives the impression that she has everything under control.

'My poor little dumplings!' she cried, and

enveloped us in a big hug. We seemed to disappear inside the huge gold-coloured robe she was wearing. She'd brought flasks of tea and biscuits. She got us all comfortable, then disappeared to find out how things were going. A few minutes later Dad appeared. He was so grey and worried looking, I was frightened. But he assured us it was all fine. He'd just let Zandra take over for a while because she seemed to know exactly what to do. He'd hardly had time for a cup of tea before a nurse came in telling him to come back. He moved, really fast. We waited, eating packet after packet of biscuits. Ages later, Auntie Zandra appeared, tears streaming down her face but a huge smile on her lips.

'Jake, Shelley, you have a beautiful little sister!'

I didn't know what to do. I didn't need to. Everyone just cried and smiled and hugged. Later, Dad came out grinning like a Cheshire Cat. Then we all tip-toed along the corridor and into a little room. There was Marilyn with a tiny little bundle of blanket. Inside it, a tiny reddish screwed-up face and lots of dark hair. It was my new sister. I couldn't believe it, Ziggy. It was so amazing to think that suddenly a new little person had appeared. I was so happy and proud.

They've called her Yvana. I don't know why, but she's very sweet. I wasn't sure how Mum was going to take the news. I told her that evening when we got home. She said she was very happy for them. It wasn't true. She was tight-lipped and quiet. She's really jealous of Marilyn. Mum never wanted Dad to leave. I think she wishes Dad was still with her and she'd just had a little baby.

The main problem was, as I expected, she went off to drown her sorrows. She wasn't back the following morning. Jake and I went to the library and then went to visit Marilyn and the baby. Jake just sat and stared at her with a silly smile on his face. He's mad on her. When we got home Mum wasn't back and the next morning there was still no sign of her.

I was getting really worried by this time. I phoned her friend Eileen, but Mum wasn't with her. I phoned the pub where she drinks but they hadn't seen her since New Year's Day. I phoned Nan and told her. She came over and made us some tea. Then she phoned the police. They didn't know anything either. Nan went off to look in all Mum's usual haunts but no one had seen her.

We got Jake to bed, then Nan and I sat and stared into space.

'Is there anything else we can do?' I said.

'Not that I can think of,' said Nan. 'We've been to all her drinking places, her friends, the bookies. And we've told the police. I can't think of anything else we can do, love.'

It was horrible, just sitting and waiting. Lots of awful possibilities came into my mind. She could have been attacked, raped, knifed, murdered, kidnapped. She could be lying helpless somewhere. We waited for ages. We watched television. We both jumped whenever the phone rang. Nan thought we should get some sleep so I tried, but every little sound in the flats or outside woke me.

Then the phone rang. I looked at my watch. It was 4.15 a.m. All I heard was Nan saying: 'Yes,' . . . 'Right,' . . . 'OK.' It was the police. They'd found Mum. They were going to bring her home.

They arrived a few minutes later. There were three of them, two big men and a woman police constable. They half dragged, half carried Mum into the house and onto the settee. She was giggling and talking rubbish. Then she started swearing and shouting obscenities at the WPC.

'Can we go into another room to talk?' said the biggest of the policemen. We went into the kitchen and Nan made them a cup of tea.

'We found her trying to break into the off-licence on Leeward Road. It wasn't a very serious attempt. She's too drunk to do much. But she's been a pain ever since.'

'How did you know who she was?' asked Nan.

'Someone at the station recognised her. He told us you'd been looking for her.'

'Are you charging her?' asked Nan.

'No, not this time.'

The WPC was looking at me.

'Have you been worried, love?' she asked.

'Yes,' I replied.

'Have you got any brothers and sisters?' she continued.

'Yes, a brother,' I replied. I didn't really want to say anything to the police.

'Have you been on your own then?' The questions went on.

'No, Nan was here,' I said. It was almost true.

The WPC turned away from me.

'Does she often do this?' she asked Nan.

Nan was silent for a minute.

'She's done it once or twice. It's not usually as bad as this,' she said quietly.

'Is she getting any help?' continued the WPC.

'No. It's only recently become a problem.'

I was getting worried. What were they going to suggest?

'The children have lots of people to turn to,' said Nan. 'Their father lives quite near, and their auntie and me. If they're worried about her they can always get help.'

'That's OK,' said the WPC, and turned to me.

'What's your name?' she said.

'Shelley.'

'Look, Shelley. You're old enough to know that your mum's got a drink problem. If things get too bad you can contact Social Services. Here's the duty number. There's always someone there.'

She gave me a piece of paper and they went. Nan and I looked at each other and sighed. We managed to get Mum, complaining loudly, to bed and then, at last, I slept.

After that, Mum was a model Mum. She told us it wouldn't happen again and spent lots of time with us. She's even learnt to use the computer.

Well, the year has started off strangely. I'm listen-

ing to *Reaching out for Life*. It seems to describe Yvana
– a new child for a new year.

Love,
Shelley

Hi Shelley,
Hang on in there.

Ziggy

Shelley Wright
16 Waterstone House
London SE6

WORDS

You really know how to hurt
Your words cut me to shreds
Like swords and knives
And thin razor blades

February 1

Dear Ziggy,
Your card took much longer to arrive than all the others have. I thought you'd forgotten me! I have all your cards in the order you've sent them on a little noticeboard in my bedroom. No one's seen them except Mum and Jake. I haven't told my friends. I'm not sure they'd believe they were really from you.

School. The term started really well. Janice was away with tonsillitis, so Charlene and Olivia were almost human. I chatted to Olivia quite a bit. Then, after Janice returned, when I said 'Hi' to Olivia she just looked away. I think Janice felt she had to re-establish her position in the class, so she was absolutely vile.

There's a girl in our class called Stacey. She's got all kinds of problems. She's really overweight. She walks in a funny shuffling way. She can't manage most of the lessons – her reading and writing aren't good. But she's really nice. She's kind and good-natured. She always helps people and looks after anyone who's hurt or upset.

Well, as soon as Janice returned she had it in for Stacey. She started writing 'Poor Stacey' and 'Can you read this, Stacey?' on the board. Then at break, she and the other two started one of their loud conversations.

'I hate fat people, don't you, Liv? she said.

'I think it's really sad, Jan,' agreed Olivia.

'Girls just shouldn't let themselves get fat, should they?' she continued. 'Of course, being fat leads to all sorts of problems.'

'What sort, Jan?' asked Charlene.

'Well, sweating and smelling are the main ones,' said Janice.

'Oh no!' said Olivia, making a face.

'That makes it very difficult for people forced to be with fat people. They suffer, of course.'

'It's not really fair, is it?' said Charlene.

'No.' Janice was really getting into her stride now.

'I think the class should protest. We have to suffer because Stacey's a greedy fat pig.'

There was silence. Stacey looked at Janice.

'I don't think that's very nice,' said Stacey nervously.

'Well, I don't think it's very nice having to look at your fat body and pink sweaty face!'

Something got into me at this point. I just couldn't stand Janice's meanness any longer.

'Well,' I said, quite quietly. 'I suggest you look at someone else instead.'

There was another tense silence.

'Did you have a suggestion to make?' asked Janice.

'Yes,' I replied. 'If you don't like looking at Stacey, don't look at her.'

'Are you trying to tell me what to do?' Her voice was rising.

'Just making a helpful suggestion,' I replied.

'Well, keep your suggestions to yourself!' Janice snarled.

'OK. So long as you keep your nasty comments about Stacey to yourself.'

There was some angry kissing of teeth from the Trio.

'First you tell me what to do. Now you tell me

what I can and can't say. Who do you think you are, Shelley?'

'No one special. Just someone who doesn't like bullies,' I answered, surprising myself at how brave I was being and how calm I sounded.

'So you're calling me a bully now,' said Janice furiously.

All three of them started to move towards me. I sat on my desk trying to look calm and unafraid. I sensed Hazel and Leonie tensing behind me and a kind of expectant hush came over the room. Janice came right up and stood in front of me, her two body-guards on either side. I looked up into Janice's face.

'I think you called me a bully, new girl!' she snarled.

'I think you were bullying Stacey. And I'm not new any more!'

I felt my heart beating very fast and every bit of me was straining to stay calm and at least look unruffled.

'Oh, I see,' the harsh, sarcastic voice continued, very close to my head. 'Now she thinks she's better than everyone else and can criticise us all!'

She waited for me to say something. I didn't.

'I think you'd better be more careful in future. I'm not a bully. I just state facts. Sometimes the truth isn't very nice to hear. Take you for example, Shelley New Girl. The truth is that your mum's a drunk. I'm sure it isn't nice to hear that – but it's a simple fact, isn't it?'

Again, I said nothing. This time it was because I was speechless. Blood was pounding through my head in a mixture of rage, embarrassment, despair. You name it, I was feeling it. Everyone in the class was listening and watching my response. I felt complete panic.

'Well,' said Janice. 'It's true isn't it?'

There was no way out. Running out of the room would have made it worse – and anyway I was unable to move. My body had frozen.

'Well,' she repeated. 'Are you going to deny that your mum's a drunk?' She said those horrible words again, slowly, enjoying each one.

I began to pull myself together. My stunned mind began to work again. I knew I couldn't deny it, but I wasn't going to publicly shame my mum either. What to do? My thoughts raced.

'I don't think,' I said very quietly, at last, 'that my mum's private life is anything to do with you.'

'It might be,' she replied. 'Like mother like daughter. You might turn out to be a very bad influence on us.'

'I doubt it,' I said.

'She's right, Janice,' said Leonie. 'It's not fair to criticise her mum. Just leave it.'

I could have kissed Leonie. Although Janice was angry at her butting in when she thought she'd got me in a corner, somehow she'd eased the pressure on me. Janice turned on her, eyes blazing.

'Now *you're* accusing me of criticising people. Didn't you hear what I said? I don't criticise. I just state facts. And here's one about you—'

'That's enough!' boomed a huge voice. It was our ferocious geography teacher. 'In your seats at once!'

So we never did find out what 'fact' Janice was going to tell us about Leonie. It was a horrible experience, Ziggy. I know what Mum's like but I don't want people talking or laughing about her. I'd already told Leonie and Hazel a bit about our problems but it wasn't something I wanted the whole class to know about. I expected whispering and maybe some comments – but I was surprised when there was neither. A couple of girls came up to me later and asked if I was all right. Stacey came and thanked me for supporting her, and some others told me they thought Janice was out of order. So, I seem to have got through yet another ordeal without major problem. I am still worried about what Janice might do or say next. And even more worried about what I might do. Twice now, I've really wanted to hit her. I know I'll get into big trouble at school and at home if I get into a fight. But I'm not sure if I can control my temper much longer. It's really hard!

The new baby is doing well. She looks adorable and Jake is still besotted with her. He's always drawing pictures or planning little story books for her when she's a bit bigger. Mum is trying to keep off the drink. It's really hard for her. She's smoking far too much and constantly drinking coffee but she's doing well. She's also got another job – in a fish and chip shop this time. The woman who runs it knows Mum quite well and she drops her off at home after work, which means she doesn't have to walk past the pub and the off-licence. She also pays her on Saturday mornings so she goes food shopping before the pubs open. It seems to be working out so far.

Last letter I was so keen to tell you about Yvana, I forgot to mention the other new member of the family. A couple of weeks ago Jake and I were woken up in the night by a noise. We couldn't work out what it was at first, then we realised it was a cat outside our window. This is pretty surprising as the flat is on the third floor. We couldn't work out how he got there, but there he was, making a terrible noise. So we took him in. He didn't seem to be hurt, just frightened. We found a tin of sardines and some evaporated milk. He wolfed them down quickly, then curled up behind the settee and went straight to sleep.

By the next morning he'd made himself quite at home. We contacted the RSPCA and the police and put a notice in the newsagent's window, but no one's claimed him. He's a big ginger-and-white cat with a funny ear and a kink in his tail. He seems to have decided that he'll live with us. Mum likes him too. We've called him Monty.

Looking forward to your new release next week.

Love,
Shelley (and Monty too)

To Shelley and
Monty.
Have fun.

Love
Ziggy

Shelley Wright
16 Waterstone House
London SE6
Inghilterra

DISAPPROVAL

Man, don't look at me that way
Man, I'm not the dirt beneath your feet
I ain't gonna hurt you
So stop your disapprovin' ways

February 15

Dear Ziggy,
The new single is fantastic, even better than the last.
And the video is so unusual – it's like watching an
exciting film, especially the roller coaster bit. The
stilt walkers were brilliant! Thanks for the card.
Monty thanks you too. He's still with us and has made
himself really at home.

I've been looking forward to writing this letter.
Most of my letters must be really depressing for you
to read, and I'm hoping this one won't be.

Last week we went on a school trip to the Science
Museum. It was organised by our science and history
teachers. I was really looking forward to it. I love
school trips, I love coach journeys and I love going

into central London. What's more I knew Janice wasn't going. She'd been ill when we had to book our places and no one had dropped out. I knew because she'd been complaining about it endlessly and trying to pressurise people into dropping out.

So there we were, three coaches full of noisy teenage girls, all laughing and squabbling and teasing each other. When Mrs Doherty and Miss McKenzie finally got us to be quiet we were given the usual lecture: 'Fasten seatbelts, no eating, no drinking, no standing up, no moving around, no shouting, no singing, no laughing.' No, that's not true, I made up the last one. The coach set off, and everyone immediately began to eat, drink, shout and sing. The teachers were busy gossiping at the front and, apart from shouting at us occasionally when it got a bit too noisy, they left us alone.

The journey was quite eventful. We stopped after about 15 minutes for Rosalind to be sick. We stopped again 15 minutes later because Rosalind had been sick again – into Shelayne's rucksack. Yuck! Then Leonie and Hazel and I compared packed lunches. The girl next to us, a big, loud, friendly girl called Heather, opened her enormous rucksack and began to pull out little parcels wrapped in silver foil. She unwrapped each one to show us, then wrapped it up neatly again: first, two jumbo sausage rolls, then two scotch eggs, then four ham sandwiches, then a tub of coleslaw, then a mini quiche, then slices of pizza, then some tomatoes, then two boiled eggs. We were already wide-eyed with astonishment when she pulled out two mini cheesecakes, a doughnut, a little apple pie, and two yogurts. But then my mouth dropped open too. When she brought out two tins of *Diet Coke* and a blackcurrant drink I thought that would be the end but *no*! Two chocolate bars, two packets of crisps and a bag of fruit gums came out next and underneath them she found another silver packet. This one contained six chicken drumsticks.

'Heather! You aren't going to eat all that are you?' asked Hazel incredulously.

'I shouldn't think so. Mum always goes OTT on picnic food. It's no good telling her there's too much. She just says, "There's always someone who has forgotten their lunch. You can give some to her",' answered Heather, sighing.

'You could feed the whole class with this, Heather,' said Leonie. 'I thought my mum had been a bit overgenerous but now my lunch looks like a tiny snack.'

'Well, if it's not enough, you know where to come,' said Heather cheerfully, loading all her parcels back into the rucksack.

When we got to the Science Museum we were all lined up and counted in through the doors. There was a huge fuss while we put our coats and bags away but, at last, we were ready, clipboards in hand. Disturbingly fat worksheets were given out. Mrs Doherty split us into groups with strict instructions to stay with our teacher. Of course we immediately ignored this and went off exploring and filling in bits of the worksheet where we could.

Have you been to the Science Museum? I really liked it. There's a good bit with space rockets you can go into. Then there's some huge machinery – so big you can't imagine how it was made or moved or used. We went upstairs to the medical section. Most of the others thought it was really sick, but I thought it was fascinating. It showed how people used to treat diseases and showed early operations and treatments, including a war-time hospital full of wounded people. The worst thing about school trips is that the wardens or whatever they're called always watch us so suspiciously. I don't know why. It isn't as if there's much in the Science Museum that school kids could steal. Everything's either too big or locked up in glass cases. One of them looked just like a Nazi officer. Little gold glasses, beady blue eyes, little moustache and really short fair hair.

'Hands off!' he said to us.

'Don't worry, we won't damage anything,' Leonie said.

'Even so,' he said suspiciously, 'hands off!'

He followed us around the whole room, checking up on us. All he said was 'Hands off!'

'I think it's his name!' said Hazel. 'Hans Hoff. You said he looked German!'

As you can imagine we all had a fit of the giggles and we ran away with 'Hans Hoff' chasing us.

At lunchtime we had to go to the schools' lunch room right down in the basement of the museum. Loads of schools must have been there before us because it was really messy. Everyone made a big fuss about the tables. Then a group from a boys' school came in and we all went quiet for a while – the boys and girls all weighing each other up. It was funny to watch. Some of the girls started preening themselves and laughing loudly and eyeing one particular group of boys. The boys began to act sophisticated and tell jokes and punch each other.

Then all hell broke loose when one horrible little twit with big ears started throwing bits of crust at a couple of girls on the next table who were laughing at him. They squealed and chucked crisps back at him. Soon, everyone else on their tables joined in and a full-scale food fight started. The teachers and the museum minders suddenly realised what was going on. Mrs Doherty started shouting but there was so much noise no one could hear her. So a huge red-faced man with a twirly moustache from the boys' school stood on a chair, blew a whistle, then bellowed in the loudest voice I've ever heard.

'Silence! Silence, this minute!'

He was pretty scary and everything quietened down. We were all marched out a table at a time while Mrs Doherty and a teacher from the boys' school tried to pacify a furious looking man in museum uniform who was waving his arms around and almost foaming at the mouth.

The worst part of the visit was at the end. We went to the shop on our way out and everyone stopped to have a look. Most of the stuff there was incredibly expensive but some people bought key rings and pens and things. Just as I was going out a huge fuss started by the key rings. I could hear one of the girls shouting.

'I didn't, I didn't,' she was saying. Then it changed to, 'I don't know how it got there. Get your hands off my bag!' There were lots of raised voices. Miss McKenzie ushered us all out of the shop but we saw Mrs Doherty and a woman disappearing with Shelayne between them. A few minutes later I discovered the woman had seen Shelayne put a key ring and a torch into her bag.

You can imagine how excited everyone was on the coach home. For a start, Mrs Doherty and Shelayne weren't on the coach and the teachers wouldn't tell us what had happened. Then, of course, the food fight was discussed in great detail. We were really noisy. We had to stop again – three times! – for Rosalind to be sick.

When we got back to school we all had to troop into the hall for a lecture on how to behave on a school trip. We were told we'd let the school down miserably and no one would ever want to take us out again.

Mum and Jake thought it was funny when I got home and told them all about it.

The best news – Mum's still got her job and she's staying off the drink most of the time. It feels like we're living a normal kind of family life for once.

Lots of love,
Shelley

Eat your dinner,
Shelley. No
throwing!

Love
Ziggy

Shelley Wright

16 Waterstone House

London SE6

KNOCK IN THE NIGHT

A hundred terrors
Skid through your head
The knock in the night
The cold sweat dread

March 1

Dear Ziggy,

Thanks for your card. I haven't thrown any food around, don't worry. If I remember rightly, I told you all about our trip in the last letter. You probably won't be too surprised to hear everything went rapidly downhill after that day.

The following week was half-term. I was looking forward to it. Jake and I had planned a few things to do and I'd organised to meet my mates on the Thursday while Jake went to see Nan. But it all went wrong. On the Saturday, Jake and I went to visit Dad and Marilyn and little Yvana. It was great. We helped change the baby and played with her while Marilyn had a bath and washed her hair. Then Dad and I made a really nice lunch with chicken and rice and peas and took the baby for a walk to the park so that Marilyn could have a rest. (She hadn't got much sleep the night before.) We fed the ducks, played on the swings and played a bit of football – the baby seemed quite happy.

Dad took us home about 10 o'clock. I got a bit worried when I saw the lights weren't on and the curtains weren't drawn.

'She must have gone out for something.' Dad tried to sound cheerful.

'I don't think she's been home, Dad. There's no curtains drawn and nothing's moved.' I wasn't so cheerful.

'I'd better wait until she gets back,' said Dad.

'Don't worry,' I told him. 'We're quite used to getting ourselves to bed. We don't get frightened any more.'

Dad looked at Jake. He knew how nervous Jake could be.

'I'll need to make sure Jakey goes to bed real soon,' he grinned and chased Jake into the bedroom laughing.

I listened to them laughing and playing and wished Dad still lived with us. He made everything more fun.

Eventually he came back and sat down with me on the settee.

'I think Jake'll soon be asleep,' he said. 'Shelley,' he asked, 'are you really all right when Mum stays out late?'

'Yes, Dad. Let's face it, I'm used to it now.'

'So you used to be frightened! Why didn't you tell me?' he continued.

'I didn't want to worry you, Dad.'

'But I'm there to be worried. That's what dads are for!' he insisted.

'Not mine,' I answered. 'Mine's there to make me smile.'

He gave me a hug.

'You just know how to get round me!' he grinned. 'Now, seriously, Shelley. If you're ever scared or Mum's drunk or anything like that, you must phone me. I can be here really quickly!'

'I know, Dad. I've been in the car with you!'

'Seriously, Shelley!'

'I know. I know. I will, Dad. If thing's get bad I know you're there but . . . '

'But what?'

'Well, it's just that I know Mum'll go mad if I phone you. Then there'll be an argument. Then she'll sulk and blame us.'

'Is it that bad?' he asked.

'Not usually,' I answered – and at that moment it felt true.

Dad eventually left when we were both in bed and he'd checked all the doors and windows. I was so tired I went to sleep very quickly.

In the middle of the night I was woken by the doorbell ringing. I was scared. It rang again. I still did nothing. Then once more.

I went to the door, afraid to open it.

'Who is it?' I asked.

'Police,' said a male voice.

'How do I know that?' I asked, thinking anyone could say they were police.

'I'll show you my ID,' said the voice. 'I'll slip it under the door.'

A little wallet came under the door – it was a police ID card. Mind you, I wouldn't know if it was a forgery. I looked at it.

'Who are you?' I asked.

'PC Peter Digby. Number 1743. Green Lane Police Station.'

'Why are you here?' I asked.

'I need to speak to you about your mum!' he said.

'Why?' I asked, for the first time worried about what might have happened. 'Is she all right?'

'Yes, but I need to talk to you about her.'

'Is she with you?' I asked.

'No, she's at the station. Can I come in? I've got a WPC here with me.'

What to do? I was frightened of what Mum might have done. I was frightened that they were coming to take us away, and I was frightened of strange people coming into our home in the middle of the night. However, I had to find out what was going on so I opened the door and let the two of them come in.

I took them into the sitting room and we sat down.

The WPC spoke first.

'I'm, sorry, love, but you need to know that your mum's been arrested.'

'Why?' I asked.

'I'm afraid she got a bit drunk and had a fight with another woman in the pub.'

'People don't always get arrested for fighting. What happened?'

'Well, it was a bit violent and lots of glasses got broken and the landlord called us.'

'But why didn't you just bring her home? You

could have.'

'That was what we were planning to do, love. But on the way she became a bit aggressive and we had to take her to the station instead.'

'What do you mean "a bit aggressive"?' I asked suspiciously.

The WPC looked at PC Digby and I saw him nod.

'The truth is your mum started a fight with the policemen who were trying to get her home. She grabbed a waste bin and hit one of them over the head. When the other officer tried to stop her she grabbed his hand and bit him, then kicked him in . . . in . . . a . . . um . . . a very tender spot. It took four of them to calm her down.'

I almost laughed. It was the way he told me – all slow and toneless like a shopping list. It all seemed so ridiculous. But it soon hit me that Mum was in serious trouble.

'What are you going to do with her?' I asked.

'We're going to keep her in the cells overnight to sleep it off. Then in the morning she'll be charged.'

'What with?'

'I don't think we've decided yet. It might be assault, might be drunk and disorderly.'

'What happens after she's charged?' I asked.

'She'll be let out on bail until her case comes up.'

I tried to take all this in. It was a bit difficult. The WPC was looking at me with a worried expression on her face.

'Are you on your own, love?' she asked.

'No, my brother's here. He's asleep.'

'Will you be OK tonight?' she continued. 'We can phone Social Services if you like.'

'No, it's OK. I don't want to disturb my brother and I'll be fine.'

I thought it would be a good idea to change the subject quickly. So I added, 'When do you think Mum will be able to come home?'

'I couldn't say at the moment – some time in the morning.'

'OK. Thanks for coming to tell us.'

'You must have been worried!' said the WPC.

'I was a bit,' I said, and smiled. I wanted them out as quickly as possible.

'Have you got other family who can help?' She was still probing!

'Yes, I've got a big family: Dad, aunts, grandmas. Don't worry.'

At last they left. I just leaned against the door. I was so relieved they'd finally gone. I realised I was also relieved to know Mum was in a police cell. At least I knew where she was and wouldn't have to worry about her being attacked or raped. We'd obviously come to the end of her latest attempt at good behaviour.

I went to check on Jake. He seemed to be fast asleep. I couldn't sleep much the rest of the night. Every time I closed my eyes I saw Mum in a cell or her hitting out at huge policemen or people coming to take Jake and me away.

Mum arrived home about midday. She looked dreadful. Her clothes were messy and torn, she had huge dark rings under her eyes. She had a bruise on one cheek and a big scratch on the other. Her lip was all swollen on one side. She looked at me and burst into tears. I gave her a hug and then fussed about getting tea and running her a bath and finding cream to put on her wounds.

After her bath she came out saying, 'Oh, Shell, I'm so sorry, I've let you down again.'

'Don't worry, Mum. You're home now.' I tried to calm her.

'But, don't you see?' she went on. 'That stupid woman was right!'

'What woman?' I asked.

'The one in the pub. The reason I got into that fight was because she started telling me I wasn't fit to be a mother and that I neglected my kids and . . . oh Shelley . . . she's right isn't she?'

'No, of course she's not, Mum. You're a lovely Mum!'

'No, she's right. I leave you alone. I go drinking. I'm hopeless.'

'You're not hopeless.' I tried to be firm.

'Shelley, I'm so frightened they'll try and take you away!' She was clutching hold of me and sobbing.

'Come on, Mum. They won't take us away. But they'll be keeping an eye on you. You must make sure you stay off the drink!'

She sobbed a bit more and then went to sleep. I needed to talk to someone about her arrest and what might happen but I wasn't quite sure who. I was full of worries. Did she need a solicitor? Did she have to report to the police station? What would she be charged with? Could she be sent to prison? How long would it be before her court case?

I knew I would have to wait for a calmer moment before talking to her about these things.

The rest of the week was grim. Mum was asleep

most of the time. When she was awake she was silent, just sitting and staring – no tears, just silence.

I hate to admit it – but I prefer it when she's drinking!

Bye for now.
Love, Shelley

Hang on in there,
Shelley.

Ziggy

Shelley Wright

16 Waterstone House

London SE6

Inghilterra

LASH OUT

You got me so confused
My head's in a daze
One day, I know
I'm gonna lash out
Lash out
Lash out at you

March 15

Dear Ziggy,
Thanks for your note – your cards have become very important to me. They keep me going, you know. Well, Mum has pulled herself together a bit. She's working a few days a week on a market stall and she's reporting to the police station as part of her bail conditions. She's still really quiet but she's trying to spend time with me and Jake. So the home front has been quietish. Nan knows about the arrest and she's given her a big talking-to. I don't think she's told anyone else.

I was a bit worried that someone at school might

have heard about Mum and make some comment. But a week went by and no one said anything. Then on the following Monday I had yet another run-in with the Trio.

Leonie and Hazel and I had just come up from dinner.

'It's a good job you have school dinners, isn't it, Shelley?' said Janice suddenly.

'Why?' I asked.

'Well, at least you'll get one meal a day when your Mum's not there,' she continued.

I could feel a cold prickling sensation in my neck and down my back.

'What do you mean?' I asked.

'Well, when your mum's banged up in prison, you'll have to fend for yourself.'

I sensed everyone's ears prick up at the mention of prison.

'I don't like you talking about my family, Janice,' I said.

'I was just expressing concern for your welfare,' she said with a sickly smile.

'Don't lie, Janice. You're not concerned about anyone's welfare. You just like to embarrass people!' I responded angrily.

She laughed. 'Seems to me it's your mum that's making you embarrassed not me!'

Suddenly, a lot of things in my head seemed to snap. I made a grab for Janice and pulled her off the desk she was sitting on. She tried to push me away, shoving me quite forcefully in the chest. I slapped her face and she grabbed my hair. I'm not sure what happened next. I know I was lashing out at her furiously – so furiously, I pushed her onto the floor. Around us, girls were screaming and shouting. More came running through the door but they all seemed to be in a different world. All I was really aware of was that I wanted to hurt this vile girl who managed to hurt me, and other people, so often.

I realised after a while that I was being pulled away. I tried to resist but I saw that Janice was being held back too. She was narrowing her eyes and spitting words out at me.

'Nobody,' I heard her say. 'Nobody gets away with attacking me!'

I was led to an office downstairs. Hazel sat with me. She didn't say anything, she just held my hand. Every so often she squeezed it. I was grateful. I didn't want to speak or listen. I felt completely dazed. I'd never done anything like that before. You imagine at

such times you might feel anger, remorse, embarrassment, even triumph! But, in fact, I felt nothing. As if
something had sucked all feelings out of me. Just
empty.

After a while, Miss McKenzie came in.

'Shelley, what on earth came over you?' she asked.

I didn't answer. I couldn't. Nothing seemed quite
real.

'Janice just went too far, Miss,' said Hazel.

'I thought you'd have learnt to ignore her stupid
remarks by now, Shelley,' said Miss McKenzie.

'You can't ignore them all. When she's cussing
your family in front of the whole class, you have to
say something.'

'You should have reported it to me and let me deal
with her.'

'Come on, Miss,' continued Hazel. 'People have
reported Janice lots of times. You've spoken to her
lots of times and has it stopped her being bitchy? No!
I'm glad Shelley thumped Janice. Maybe if more
people had done it in the past she wouldn't be so
horrible now.'

'Hazel, you know it's never right to hit people,'
Miss McKenzie seemed surprised.

'On the whole, yes. But where bullies are

concerned, I think it does them good to get a taste of their own medicine sometimes!'

Miss McKenzie was silent and thoughtful. She gazed at me.

'Are you hurt, Shelley?' she asked, concerned.

'I don't think so,' I replied. I couldn't really feel anything.

At that point Mrs Doherty came in.

'Shelley, you're in serious trouble! Now, first things first. Are you injured?'

'I don't think so,' I repeated.

'Well, I'm not so sure. That looks like a bruise on your cheek, you've got scratches on your arm and I think you've lost some hair.'

I felt my cheek. She was right. Miss McKenzie went to fetch some ice and antiseptic wipes.

'Now, I want you and Hazel to sit quietly and write down what happened, from start to finish.'

'She's not going to be excluded, is she?' asked Hazel.

'I don't know yet. When I've got all the details, I'll discuss it with the Deputy Head. Now, the sooner you write your accounts the sooner I can let you know the outcome.'

We spent ages writing down what had happened.

In the middle, Miss McKenzie came to do her Florence Nightingale act.

At last we finished. Hazel was sent back to class and I sat opposite Mrs Doherty as she read out the accounts. A girl brought in some more pieces of writing and she read those too. I watched her, but she showed no clear reaction. Then she stopped, leaned back in her chair and stared hard at me.

'What impression do you think I've had of you up until today?' she asked.

'I've no idea,' I replied.

'I'll tell you. Intelligent, hard-working, responsible, mature, thoughtful.' She paused and looked at me again. 'Are you those things, Shelley?'

'I'm not sure. Some of them. Put all together it sounds a bit too good to be me.'

'I don't think it is too good to be you, Shelley. You've made a very good impression. Now, what went wrong today?'

'I flipped. I've managed to keep my temper with Janice up to now and that's been hard enough. Today, I couldn't take her any more. Something snapped.'

'I've read the accounts, Shelley. She was teasing you about your mother going to prison, wasn't she?'

'Yes.'

'And is there any truth in this? Is your mother in trouble?'

I didn't want to tell her. But I couldn't get out of answering such a direct question.

'Shelley, you can answer me without being disloyal. I don't report to the police or discuss your home life with other staff!'

'Yes, she is in trouble . . . she was arrested during half-term. She . . .'

Once I'd said it, I felt a kind of wave overtake me. I burst into tears and blurted out all the details. Mrs Doherty just sat listening and passing me tissues. I seemed to go on for hours and then suddenly stopped – there were no more words, no more tears. I was all cried out, all talked out. I watched to see her response.

'Shelley, you've been bearing a huge burden. Does anyone else know?'

'No, only my nan.'

'What about your dad?'

'I don't want to tell him yet. He'll get really worried and have a go at Mum. And he's got a new baby to look after at the moment.'

'OK. What about other sources of help?'

'You mean you're going to tell Social Services?'

I panicked, suddenly afraid of what I'd said and done.

'No, Shelley. I'm not going to tell anyone. But there may be a point at which you need some help and advice. I just want you to know you can talk to Miss McKenzie or me, and if you want we can put your name down to see the school counsellor. It's all confidential!'

I thought for a minute.

'Does my mum need to know?'

'No, it's confidential and unofficial.'

'And nothing to do with Social Services?'

'Nothing.'

'OK, I'll do it.'

'Well, that reassures me a bit, Shelley. Now, let's get down to business. Is Janice always nasty?'

'Yes.'

'To you in particular or to everyone?'

'Almost everyone except her two mates. Recently, it seems to be me in particular.'

'And how do you think she knew about your mum?'

'I don't know. I suppose someone she knows must have been in the pub that night. She always seems to be able to find out people's secrets.'

'Well, I do understand your anger with her and I do know how unpleasant Janice can be. That may explain your actions but you know as well as I do that it doesn't excuse them. Your response was violent and wrong.'

'I know,' I said sulkily.

'Now I'm going to see the Deputy. I'm going to recommend that you are treated leniently, Shelley. I will have to explain some of the background. But you don't need to worry about it going any further.'

I obviously didn't look very convinced because she added, 'Shelley, I spend half my time hearing details of people's private lives. So do other staff. We are used to keeping things to ourselves. Sometimes we can't but that's when we're told of a crime that we have to report or if we think a pupil's being hurt or neglected. These things don't apply in your case, so stop worrying.'

I wasn't quite convinced but she smiled and went off. I sat staring around the little office, wondering what was going to happen to me. After a while, Miss McKenzie came in.

'Come on, Shelley. I've been asked to take you to

Miss Tiptree's office.'

I got up and followed her. I was terrified. Miss Tiptree is really frightening. She's very tall and thin and always wears dark suits. She's got black hair cut really short and black-rimmed glasses. She talks very quietly but you know she means what she says. She passes through the school in a kind of quiet bubble because when we see her we automatically lower our voices and stop whatever nonsense we're involved in. She reminds me of a nun, a very stern nun.

Anyway, I've never spoken to her before or been taken to her office.

Miss McKenzie squeezed my arm when we got to the door. 'Good luck,' she whispered, and I went in.

'Stand over here, Shelley,' the quiet, clear voice said. 'I've heard the whole story. I'm pleased that your form teacher and Mrs Doherty speak so highly of you.'

She stared hard at me.

'My final decision is conditional, Shelley. If you can give me an undertaking not to respond violently to Janice's provocation in future, I'm prepared to view this as a first offence and let you off with a severe warning, a week in my detention and a letter home.

The alternative is a three-day exclusion – all official and on your file. What do you say?'

I was trying to take this in. She spoke quickly. I felt like I was in court and I didn't know what to say.

'Can I ask what you're going to do with Janice?' I stuttered.

'A good question. I intend to offer Janice something similar.'

'But—'

'Don't interrupt me, Shelley. We are aware that Janice is a bully. In her case, I intend to see her mother to discuss this. I will refer her to our new bullying counsellor for intensive sessions and give her the same detention as you.'

'And what about *her* undertaking not to be so nasty. I can't promise not to get angry if she continues to say such horrible things, can I?'

'You're right, Shelley. I have considered that too. She is to make a similar undertaking and Miss McKenzie will be asking the class to monitor Janice's behaviour.'

I thought for a minute. I'd expected some punishment – but I must admit I had no idea they'd treat the problem so seriously. 'I will undertake what you ask. And thank you . . . both of you.'

'You don't need to thank either of us, Shelley, but I appreciate you doing so. Now listen carefully. I dislike repeating myself. We feel you are a fine pupil and could do extremely well. We intend to help you to do that. However, this has revealed a weakness in your character – a lack of control that must be remedied. I must emphasise that such behaviour must not be repeated. I only show leniency once. Is that clear?'

'Yes, Miss Tiptree.'

'Good. Now, go and sit outside the office and wait for a letter. You are to take it home to your mother. You must return the slip at the bottom with her signature. And tomorrow after school you will meet me in C15 for detention. Now you may go.'

I left, a little dazed and confused by Miss Tiptree and her speedy efficiency. I collected the letter and took it home to Mum.

'This is all my fault, Shelley,' she said when she'd read it. 'I'm so sorry.'

That was all she said. She kissed me and went into the kitchen sniffing.

I'm sorry to burden you with the details of yet another crisis in my life, Ziggy, but as you know, I'm trying to be honest and it helps me to think things

139

through clearly when I write them down.

Thank you for being there,

Love,
Shelley

Keep it cool,
Shelley.
Hang on in there.

Ziggy

Shelley Wright

16 Waterstone House

London SE6

PULL THROUGH

If I think hard enough
If I pray hard enough
I know you can make it
Pull through, baby, pull through

April 1

Dear Ziggy,
I'm going to try and keep this letter cheerful. Thanks so much for your card.

As you can imagine, I was terrified of going into school after the fight with Janice but I needn't have worried. Everyone in the class was really kind and concerned. Janice was away from school for a week and we had some class discussions about monitoring and dealing with bullying.

When Janice did come back she gave a lot of dirty looks and the Trio did a lot of whispering but she kept a low profile.

By that time most of the class had a new interest. Leonie is going to have a party – a party with a difference. Leonie has a brother, Danny, who is a year older than her and their mum is letting them have a joint party. She's hired a hall and a disco and it's going to be from 8 to 11.

Nearly everyone in our class is going and, more importantly, so are most of the boys in Danny's class. I've seen Danny with some of his friends and a few of them are quite good looking. Lots of girls in our class are far more into boys than I am. They've had boyfriends and endlessly discuss who they fancy and who they don't. So, there's been massive discussions of all the male guests who'll be at the party. Even without getting too involved in the conversations, I seem to have learnt their names, height, skin colour, taste in clothes, taste in music and the general impression they've given.

My main worry has been whether I'll actually get there. Mum said I could go if I got a lift home. I persuaded Dad to give me a lift home and, just in case Mum decided on an evening out, I arranged for Jake to go to Nan's. So that was all sorted out. Next problem: what to wear.

This, too, has been the topic of endless debate at school. I looked in my wardrobe and decided I couldn't go. There was nothing I could possibly wear. I asked Mum. She likes clothes and some of her clothes are really nice. The only problem is she hasn't really noticed that she's put on weight. So nearly everything she wears seems a bit tight. Anyway, she suggested I borrow a little sleeveless top of hers that's silvery black and wear it with a black skirt. I really liked the top but settled on trousers instead – better for dancing. So I was happy. But I needed to consider my hair.

Well, my mum's hopeless with my hair so I went to visit Auntie Zandra to ask if she'd help. She was thrilled.

'Look what I've just bought,' she said, and held up a magazine called *Big, black, beautiful hair.* 'Come on, let's get some ideas!'

We spent a happy hour browsing through the magazine. You should have seen some of the styles. There was one that looked like the horns on a buffalo, one that looked like a hairy dog and one that looked like spoons standing up all over the model's head. We finally decided on one with little plaits that go across the head in a zig-zig pattern and form little hanging plaits at the back.

'But you can't do that, can you?' I asked Zandra.

'No, but I know someone who can!' And she was

soon on the phone to her friend Doreen who agreed to come and do my hair the day before the party.

'But it'll cost a lot of money!' I said.

'Don't you worry about that,' said Zandra. 'That'll be my contribution to your party.'

I gave her a hug.

'Now, you don't get something for nothing, Shelley,' she grinned. 'You go and keep Marlon occupied for an hour or so. OK?'

It was no hardship. Marlon's at the age when he's interested in everything – so he was easy to please. And to tell you the truth I like playing with PlayDo and Plasticine and drawing big pictures with wax crayons. I also like building blocks!

I was just beginning to enjoy myself when Zandra came in looking really upset.

'What's the matter?' I asked.

'Oh, Shelley, that was your uncle on the phone. It's bad news. I . . .' She burst into tears.

'What on earth's happened?' I asked, hundreds of horrible possibilities flashing through my mind.

'It's Nanny. She's been rushed into hospital. They think she's had a stroke!'

I wasn't sure exactly what a stroke was but I knew it was serious and I could see Zandra was really worried.

'Is there anything we can do?' I asked, feeling helpless.

'Yes,' said Zandra, and almost instantly she stopped crying and started organising.

'I'll phone Fluff and tell him I'm off to Manchester. I'll have to take Marlon with me because Fluff's at a conference.'

She went out to make phone calls, leaving Marlon staring after her with big worried eyes. I tried to cheer him up and started playing again but it was hard work. Both of us knew something serious had happened. I just kept on thinking over and over again, 'Please don't let her die, God, please don't let her die!'

I haven't mentioned Nanny to you before because I haven't seen her very often since I started writing. You see, she lives in Manchester so I only get to see her when she visits London or I visit Manchester.

I used to see her much more often. Jake and I used to stay with her during the summer holidays but we didn't last year because she was ill – she had shingles.

She's a lovely lady. She's very small and always wears smart dresses, or a suit and hat on Sunday. She's quiet and kind and very religious. She's always attending church or prayer group or bible class or choir.

Last time we saw her, at Christmas, she seemed smaller and more frail than before. Dad said that was because of the shingles. I couldn't bear to think of her being ill in hospital, and I know people don't always recover completely from strokes. Nanny taught us all kinds of little prayers when we were younger. That day when I was playing with Marlon, I went through all of them in my head.

After hours on the telephone, Zandra came back to tell me what was happening. Dad was going to drive up to Manchester with her, leaving Marlon with Marilyn until his daddy, Fluff, returned from the conference.

I volunteered to help Marilyn look after the two little ones while they were away. Zandra gave me a big kiss, then dashed upstairs to pack Marlon's and her things. By the end of the day Marlon and I had succeeded in building a tower as tall as me – and peopled it with lots of creatures made from dough. It was great fun!

As you can imagine, the few days after that phone call were really worrying. Jake and I went round to help Marilyn every day after school. We managed to keep Marlon occupied and help her with the baby. Every time Dad phoned, he sounded worried and tired. Nanny didn't seem to be responding to them nor to any treatment.

I began to dread the phone ringing – in case it was bad news. Then, on the Tuesday evening, we were all eating pasta at Marilyn's when the phone rang.

Jake and I were both straining to hear the conversation but Marilyn had closed the door. Even the baby was silent. Then Marilyn suddenly shouted out, 'Shelley, come here.'

I rushed out into the hall.

She was smiling. I grabbed the phone.

'Dad, what's happened?' I asked.

'Good news, Shelley. Nanny's not only opened her eyes today but she's also talking!'

'Great news,' I said, tears filling my eyes. 'Is she going to get completely better?'

'We don't know yet. She still can't move her right arm and leg, but that may come with time. But she's definitely on the mend.'

'I'm so pleased, Dad. I've been praying for her you know!'

'I know you have, Shelley. And I hear you've really helped Marilyn. Well done. Zandra and I will be home tomorrow, now we know she's out of danger. I'll see you and Jake then.'

It was such a relief. I'd thought about Nanny such a lot and I couldn't decide which would be more unbearable – her dying, or her being alive but unable to walk or speak or anything. I've read about people who live like that for years. It frightens me. What goes on in their minds? Are they thinking the same as the rest of us but can't express it or are their minds paralysed too? How could we find out? I can't bear to think of what it would be like to be able to think and feel but not be able to communicate. You'd just hear people around you talking as if you didn't exist! Well, you can see that Nanny's stroke has got me thinking lots of morbid things. I can't tell you how happy I am now that she's getting better. I just hope Dad will take us to see her in the holidays.

When Dad came back, Jake and I spent more time at home again. I think Mum's been feeling a bit left out, because we've been with Marilyn so much. Anyway, good news! Mum's still got her job and she's been trying hard not to drink too much.

We've got a week to go at school, then it's the party and then it's the Easter holidays. I just hope you're going to be on the *Easter Pop Xtravaganza*.

I'll be keeping my fingers crossed.

Please keep sending the cards.
Love,
Shelley

Party on,
Shelley!

Love
Ziggy

Shelley Wright
16 Waterstone House
London SE6

PARTY

Let's see you shake, shake, shake,
Let's see you slide, slide, slide,
Let's see you move real fast
Come on let's party!

April 15

Dear Ziggy,

Thanks for the card and thanks for the photo. I watched *Xtravaganza*. The band was fantastic. It was so exciting to see you do a big live concert like that. I switched off all the lights, turned up the sound, and pretended I was really there!

Well, I've got a lot to tell you. Everyone was ridiculously excited by the day of the party, especially since it was the beginning of the holidays as well. Dad gave me some money to buy a present so I bought Leonie a pretty little necklace and some hair mascara (purple) that she's been going on about for ages.

The night before the party I went round to Zandra's to meet her friend Doreen. I'd love you to meet Doreen. Even to do my hair she was dressed like a pop star. She's very tall – about six foot – and big all over. She had her hair all piled on top of her head and wore platform heels, so she looked even taller. She had huge earrings, nose and eyebrow rings, armfuls of bracelets, and dozens of chains round her neck. She had a tight-fitting black T-shirt with a low neckline and very tight trousers with a wide gold belt. She also had golden eye make-up and the brightest lipstick I'd ever seen. She was wonderful. She spent about an hour and a half doing my hair and the same again doing Zandra's, and we spent the whole time giggling. She told us stories and jokes and described some of the weird and wonderful people she's met. She sometimes works on video and film sets so she's got a store of stories about famous people. Not only did we have a lot of fun but my hair looked fantastic. I hardly recognised myself. And Zandra looked like a model when hers was finished.

On the day of the party Mum helped me with my make-up. When, at last, I was ready, Mum told me I looked beautiful and gave me a big hug. Then she walked with me to Hazel's house. I'd arranged to go with Hazel because I didn't want to arrive by myself.

Hazel's dad dropped us off and we stood a bit nervously outside the hall. We could hear the beat of disco music coming from inside.

'Come on,' said Hazel. 'We can't stand around out here forever!'

In we went. For a few moments I could hardly see. It seemed very dark and the flashing coloured lights were quite dazzling. Leonie rushed up to us, followed by a group of other girls. 'Hazel, Shelley, you look great! Shelley, the hair, it's really nice. It must have taken hours. Come in and say hello to everyone.' We were surrounded by a sea of chattering, most of which was impossible to hear because of the noise of the music. Once I'd got used to it I could see that the hall was in two sections. At one end were some tables and chairs and in the midst of them all were two huge tables groaning under the weight of plates and plates of food and a massive collection of bottles and cartons of drink. The other end of the room had been cleared for dancing, with the DJ and his lights and equipment in one corner. There were balloons and streamers everywhere. It was exactly how I'd imagined. This was the first party I'd been to with girls and boys and dancing, and I wasn't quite sure what would happen.

At first, everyone hung around in groups, girls one side, boys the other! Once we'd all seen what our friends were wearing and had gossiped and admired each other for a while, our attention turned to the boys. And it was clear that their attention was on the girls. No one danced for ages. The boys messed about, pushed and shoved each other and laughed ridiculously loudly. I think we were doing the same – giggling and gossiping.

Then, suddenly, everything kind of changed tempo. The DJ put on ZB4 – you know, that really fast bouncy track. It's really popular and everyone rushed forward and started dancing to it. I think they'd all been practising the dance all week! I know I had. After that there was non-stop dancing – girls together and boys together at first but soon boys and girls started dancing together. I was really having fun when Hazel said, 'Look at Joel, over there, he keeps looking at you!'

I knew who Joel was. I'd seen him a few times before and I'd always thought he seemed very nice. I looked across and he seemed to be absorbed in a conversation with Danny so I told Hazel not to be so stupid. I will admit to you that from then on I did keep glancing towards him. He danced very well and he's a really good-looking boy, but I'd always got the impression he was quite shy. He did smile across at me but then he was dancing with some other girl.

'Look,' I said to Hazel. 'You're wrong. He's dancing with someone else!'

'You're not watching carefully enough,' she replied. 'He didn't have any choice. She went up and grabbed him.'

I risked another glance and thought he did look a bit uncomfortable with this girl but I tried not to think about it. Instead, I went off to get a drink.

'Could you pour me one, too?' said a voice behind me as I was pouring some *Coke*. I turned round.

It was him!

'Of course,' I said.

I was really pleased it was dark. I'm sure my face must have been all flushed. I managed to spill quite a lot on the table but eventually I was able to hand him a paper cup, almost full of *Coke*.

'Cheers,' he said, and smiled.

We drank a bit.

'You're Shelley, aren't you? I've seen you with Leonie a couple of times. My name's Joel.'

'Nice to meet you, Joel,' I said, knowing it sounded stupid as soon as I'd said it.

'You look different tonight,' he went on. 'It's your hair. It really suits you.'

'Thanks,' I stammered out, wishing I could say something more . . . more meaningful.

'Do you like this track?' he asked.

'No I don't. Do you?' I managed.

'No. That bit there really grates on my nerves somehow. It sounds like a dog whining!'

'It does, doesn't it,' I agreed. 'But I think it's her voice that annoys me most. She sounds like one of those talking dolls.'

We both laughed and I was really pleased that he had the same ideas as me. I'd never understood why people liked that song so much. It was that Raggamuffin's song *Eloise*.

We chatted for about half an hour about music and we seemed to have very similar tastes. And guess what, Ziggy, he's a fan of yours! So he can't be that bad can he?

Then when your new single came on he took my hand and led me over to the dance section. We danced together for the rest of the evening, with just a few stops to cool off or have a drink. We managed to talk quite a bit even though the music was really loud and we had to shout in each other's ear. That was how I discovered he even smelt nice too – which was different to a few of the boys who were there that evening, I can tell you!

The evening went so quickly. Suddenly the DJ was announcing that this was going to be the last record. I couldn't believe it. I didn't want the party to end. I was really enjoying being with Joel. I think he must have sensed my panic – or he must have been feeling the same himself. He took my hand and led me a bit further away from the speakers so we could hear each other more easily. He didn't let go of my hand. He turned round to face me and put his other hand on my arm.

'I've . . . I've really enjoyed being with you, Shelley. I was wondering . . . if we could see each other again?'

My heart was racing. He had this worried look on his face as if he was frightened I'd tell him to get lost.

'I'd like that, Joel,' I said – or at least that's what I'd planned to say but my mouth went all dry and I started coughing and choking. We both started giggling idiotically and he patted me on the back to stop me coughing. Then he gave me a little hug.

'Shall I phone you?' he asked.

'OK. I won't be at home tomorrow, but I will be next week.'

He got out a pen and I wrote my phone number on his hand – and he wrote his on mine. Then I noticed Dad trying to look inconspicuous by the door.

'My dad's arrived,' I said.

'Am I allowed to meet him?' Joel asked.

'Of course!' I said, a bit surprised. I thought boys tried to avoid meeting girls' parents at all costs. I took him over. I could see Dad looking at him very carefully.

'Hello, Dad,' I said.

'Hi, Shelley. Good party?' he said, eyes still on Joel.

'Yes, great. Dad, this is my friend Joel.'

Joel put out his hand.

'Pleased to meet you,' he said very politely, and they shook hands.

'I'd better go and say goodbye,' I said, suddenly realising that I'd deserted my friends. Feeling a bit mean, I left Joel with my dad while I dashed around saying goodbye to everyone. Of course they all had some remark to make about Joel so it was a bit embarrassing. I made my getaway only to discover that Dad had offered Joel a lift home and he'd accepted.

So, a few minutes later, there we were in the back of Dad's car while Dad was doing that parent-thing of asking Joel lots of questions about school and his parents and brothers and sisters. Joel was really polite and gave all the right answers. Secretly, I was quite pleased because it meant I found out quite a lot about him too. All too soon we were at his house. He grabbed my hand and squeezed it.

'I'll phone you, Shelley,' he said, and, thanking my dad for the lift, he got out of the car. As we drove off he waved and winked.

'Well, well, well,' said Dad.

'What's that meant to mean?' I said, laughing.

'A boyfriend!' he said.

'Dad, I've only just met him!'

'But you like him, don't you?' he answered.

'Yes, but don't start marrying me off yet. I've only spent a couple of hours with him. Anyway, what did you think of him?'

'He seemed a decent kind of boy,' he said thoughtfully.

'I can sense a "but" coming up!' I said.

Dad laughed. 'No, Shelley. I really did like him. It's

just a bit of a shock to find my little girl's old enough to have a boyfriend. It makes me feel old.'

I laughed. 'You are old, Dad!'

Well, that's the story of the party.

Lots of love,
Shelley

Keep on dancing,
Shelley.

Love
Ziggy

Shelley Wright

16 Waterstone House

London SE6

SAFE

Let me hold you in
My arms
Keep you safe
Let me kiss away
Your tears
Keep you safe

May 1

Dear Ziggy,
Thanks for your card. I realised when I got it that I'd spent the whole of my last letter telling you about Joel and the party and didn't have time for any other details. I'll try to remedy that this time.

Where to begin? Well, I'll start with the best news. Nanny's out of hospital and beginning to walk with a stick. Even better, Dad took Jake and I up to see her and we had a really nice time. The weather was warm and we took her out a few times and she was really pleased to see us.

Back at home life's been interesting. Mum's been

working longer hours at the market because of the Easter holidays but she is keeping out of the pub. She's still quieter than usual but it's better than her being drunk! She also had to go back to court again but not for the proper trial yet.

Well, my holidays, as you might imagine, didn't turn out as I'd expected. I'd thought Jake and I would have a quiet time going to the park or the library or playing on the computer. I did know I had to do lots of revision because we have exams as soon as we get back to school.

Anyway, the Monday after the party Joel phoned and asked if I'd like to go bowling with Danny and Leonie. I asked if it would be all right if Jake came along. I thought Joel might not be keen, but he suggested he bring his little brother as well so they could keep each other company. It was great. I'd only been once before – it's really good fun. I like the noise the ball makes when it rolls along and I like watching the machine take the skittles up and down.

I was really nervous about seeing Joel again. I kept on thinking what if I don't like him? What if he isn't as nice as he seemed at the party? I was shaking when we arrived at the bowling centre. Leonie and Danny were already there. So of course my next panic was:

would he turn up? He did, about two minutes later, with his brother. He came straight over to me, smiling, and introduced his little brother, Scott. He and Jake were both a bit shy at first but soon they were chatting away. I felt a bit shy too. It's all so different when you meet again in the daytime. At parties it's dark and you have to get close to hear each other speak and to dance. So you're kind of forced together in a way. This time, meeting in front of Jake and Leonie, I was terrified that we wouldn't have anything to say to each other.

In fact, it was fine. To begin with we were all busy organising ourselves – tickets, changing our shoes, and finding our lane. Then Joel offered to go and get us all drinks and crisps. He gave me a sideways look and I volunteered to go with him. Once away from the others, he tucked his arm in mine.

'I'm glad you could come out today,' he said, smiling.

I sensed he was as nervous as I felt.

'It's a really good idea,' I answered. 'I haven't been bowling for ages.'

'Did you enjoy the party on Saturday?' he asked, hesitantly.

'It was great,' I said. I wanted to make him less

nervous, but I was not sure how to say things. 'It was nice . . . being with you, Joel,' I blurted out.

He stopped walking and turned round to me.

'Do you mean that, Shelley?' he asked, very seriously.

'Of course I do,' I told him.

There was a moment's silence and I wondered what on earth he was going to do or say. He looked so thoughtful.

Then suddenly, it was as if a light was turned on. He smiled, his eyes shone and he put his hands on my shoulders and, leaning forward, kissed me on the forehead.

'I'm so pleased, Shelley. I kept on worrying that maybe you just put up with me at the party – but I've been thinking about you all the time since we met.'

We stood grinning foolishly at each other for a while and then we kissed! Now, writing this letter, it seems such a simple thing to write those two words. But at the time, what happened was not simple. I knew I was going to kiss him – not because any thoughts went through my head but because something stronger and unstoppable was happening somewhere inside me. It was instinctive. Thoughts didn't come into it. I could see in Joel's eyes that the same thing was happening to him. It was a soft, warm, gentle kiss. Afterwards, we stood surprised and shaken. I could feel my heart beating so fast and so loud, I thought he must be able to hear it. He stroked my hair and I took hold of his other hand and clutched it tightly.

'Hey, Joel, how you doin'?' said a voice behind me.

It was as if a hypnotist had clicked his fingers to call us out of a trance. The world around us suddenly came into being again – noisy, busy and harsh.

'Oh, Lloyd! I'm just fine, what about you?'

'Great. I was just leaving when I noticed you. Are you going to introduce me to your girl?'

Lloyd was looking at me very closely.

'Yeh, of course. This is Shelley, my . . . my girl-friend. Shelley, this is a school friend, Lloyd.'

'Hi,' I said, and Lloyd smiled. He opened his mouth to say something but his mates shouted to him to hurry up.

'Sorry, got to go!' he said. 'You look after him, Shelley. He's a great guy!'

And Lloyd was off.

'Joel,' I said, and he looked a bit worried. 'I think it's time you and your . . . girlfriend bought those drinks. Otherwise we're going to be in big trouble.'

He laughed, grabbed my hand, and we ran over to the café.

Since then, I've seen Joel almost every day. We've been to the cinema and the park and this last week we've been to the library every day to revise. It's not very easy. The first time, Jake was playing on the computer and Joel and I went and sat together. It was hopeless. I just couldn't concentrate with him there. I wanted to talk to him or make him laugh or just watch him. We decided we'd have to sit at separate tables!

I've been to his house and met his parents and brothers – and his dog, Marg. He's met Dad and Marilyn and Mum now. They all like him.

I was really nervous the first time I invited him home. He'd been there to pick me up a few times but Mum wanted him to come for tea so she could talk to him. I was terrified. She insisted he come to Sunday tea. Sunday is Mum's worst day. She's often sleeping off a hangover or going out for 'a little drink' at lunch time and not returning until midnight.

So I told Joel all about Mum's drink problem, just in case. He told me about his uncle who's a heroin addict, and I felt better. It was nice just to share it. And Mum was great. She didn't go anywhere near the pub. She cooked a lovely roast and apple crumble and she and Joel chatted like old mates. Now she thinks he's wonderful. And, as a matter of fact, so do I.

There was only one really bad moment this holiday. The other evening Joel and I were going to see a film. We were in the queue outside the cinema when I heard a familiar voice behind me. It was Janice. I didn't look round but I could hear that there was a whole group of people with her, shouting and laughing. I whispered to Joel not to look round and warned him what a cow she was.

Of course she'd seen us. She'd obviously already bought her ticket. She called out my name. I ignored her and held Joel's hand tightly. She came over.

'Hello, Shelley, how nice to see you!' she said with complete insincerity.

'Hello, Janice,' I replied.

But her interest was no longer on me.

'And if it isn't Joel!' she continued.

'Hello, Janice,' said Joel pleasantly.

'Are you two – you know – seeing each other then?' she asked.

'Yes,' said Joel, with a fixed but not very friendly smile.

I was a bit surprised. I didn't know he knew her.

'How sweet!' said Janice in her most unpleasant tone.

Then she turned to me.

'Oh dear, Joel, I think you've upset Shelley. Didn't you tell her we go back a long way?'

Joel snorted. 'Shelley and I have better things to talk about, Janice. It was nice seeing you but—'

'Oh dear,' she cut in. 'You're trying to get rid of me! That's not very friendly. I wanted a good chat. There's so many interesting things I could tell you about your new girlfriend, Joel.'

'I doubt it,' said Joel, trying hard to stay calm.

'Well, I think it's great that you're so protective. She'll need protection when her mum goes to prison, won't she?'

I could feel myself getting angrier and angrier. I wanted to spit at her. Joel held my hand tight and held on to my other arm.

'Thanks for your concern, Janice – but we don't have any secrets.'

'Oh, really – don't be too sure of that!' She grinned nastily.

Fortunately, at that point her friends called out to her and, smiling her vicious smile, she went into the cinema.

I was so full of rage I was almost crying. We left the cinema queue and went home. No one was there. Jake was at Dad's and Mum had gone out. I burst into tears and told Joel all about Janice and how she'd behaved at school. He put his arms round me and listened. I felt better when I'd finished the story.

'But how does she know you?' I asked, a little hint of jealousy in my mind.

'You know the uncle I told you about?'

'The junkie one?'

'Yes. Well, he lives next door to Janice and her mum. When I was younger I used to play with Janice when I went to visit. My uncle and her mum had some kind of relationship at the time.'

'And now?'

'I don't visit any more. Dad doesn't like me going there. But I think they've fallen out now. There's been some row between them.'

'Did you like her, Joel?'

'No, she's always been like that. Watch her, Shelley. She and her mum are dangerous. My dad thinks it was her mum who got Uncle Derek into heroin in the first place.'

'So she's into drugs!' I was surprised.

'She's into anything. Her mum's got some very

heavy friends, Shelley. Try and stay well clear of her.'

I'd always been nervous of Janice. Now, the thought of 'heavy friends' filled me with fear. It was comforting to snuggle up to Joel and watch a video that I'd seen a hundred times before. He made me feel safe and warm and protected.

I hope you're safe and happy.

Love,

Shelley

Stay safe,
Shelley.

Love
Ziggy

Shelley Wright

16 Waterstone House

London SE6

FEAR

Fear is a chill that
Goes right through you,
Fear is a knife through your heart,
Fear is a child
Alone in the night

May 15

Dear Ziggy,
Thanks for your card. I sometimes think it would be great to actually meet you one day so I could tell you how much your cards have meant to me. It never seems to sound as sincere on paper.

As you can imagine, I wasn't keen for the holidays to end. It meant school, exams, Janice, and, worst of all, not seeing so much of Joel. Both his parents and mine told us we couldn't see each other every day once school began again. So we agreed we would spend one weekday evening together and then see each other at the weekend.

Well, it wasn't so bad going back to school. It was

great to see my friends. Of course they all wanted to know everything about Joel. I got lots of teasing and questions. Unfortunately, Janice was there and made it her business to say something.

'Hello, Shelley,' she said with a sarcastic tone and forced smile. 'It was so nice to bump into you and Joel in the holidays.'

I didn't say anything. I was waiting to see what else was coming.

'It must be nice for someone like you to have a boyfriend. It's so *sweet*!'

There was silence.

'I suppose Joel told you how close he and I are?' she added.

I managed to keep my mouth shut.

She didn't, of course.

'Mind you, I was a bit surprised. No offence, Shelley, but I thought Joel would have better taste.'

This time I couldn't keep quiet. But I did keep my temper.

'Oh, don't worry, Janice. I couldn't possibly take offence. I'll just pass on your comments to Joel.'

'You do that,' she said and, turning back to her mates, she continued in a loud whisper, 'She ought to make the most of it. He's bound to get sick of the

171

boring little tart pretty quickly.'

I pretended not to hear. Actually, I wasn't really annoyed because I got the feeling Janice really was jealous. She didn't say much else directly but I've been getting even more dirty looks and vicious comments.

Joel advised me to just ignore her.

Last Wednesday evening he came round and we did some revising together. I'd told Mum he was coming and I thought she'd be there but she didn't get back from work. After Jake had gone to bed Joel and I did some more revision. We were both tired but he didn't want to go home and leave me on my own. We ended up watching some ancient movie on the television. I must have dropped off to sleep.

The next thing I knew someone was screaming. I opened my eyes and saw Mum swaying in front of me.

'You dirty little cow!' she screamed, her voice thick with drink, her words slurred.

'The minute I turn my back you two are on the settee doing God knows what!'

Joel stood up and began to argue.

'What we were doing was revising, then—'

'Spare me the details, you scum. I thought you

were a nice boy. I thought you were different. But you're all the same. Only after one thing!'

'For God's sake, Mum! What are you suggesting? Joel and I were watching a film while we waited for you to come home. Joel—'

'Watching a film! Who do you think you're fooling? You were curled up asleep together. I know what you've been up to!'

'We haven't done anything we shouldn't have,' said Joel. 'Look, we've got all our clothes on, we've got our books with us.'

'Anyone can put their clothes back on!' Mum shouted.

I looked at her in despair. I was so embarrassed. I hadn't wanted Joel to see her drunk. That was bad enough. But for her to make these kind of accusations, when we'd behaved completely innocently, was beyond bearing.

'Mum, please don't be so unfair. The only reason Joel's here is because he wouldn't leave me by myself. He was really tired but he still wouldn't go home until you got back. Now look at the thanks he gets.'

'Thanks! You must think I was born yesterday. Don't play the innocent with me, Shelley. I just don't know how you could behave like that with Jake asleep in the next door room.'

'Mum, for the last time, we *haven't* done anything wrong!'

She stared hard at me, then sunk into a chair and took a bottle from her bag. I turned to Joel, tears of anger and resentment blinding me.

'She's home now, Joel. You'd better go.'

He took my hand. He was going to say something else to Mum but we both saw her eyes begin to glaze over. I went to the door with him.

'I'm so sorry, Joel,' I said, trying unsuccessfully not to cry.

He held me close. 'Don't apologise. It's not you, it's your mum. Is she often like that?'

'She hasn't been for a while. I just hope this isn't the start of a new phase. She'll be full of apologies in the morning.'

'With a bit a luck, she might even have forgotten the whole thing,' he said.

He opened the door and kissed me goodnight.

'Hang on in there, Shelley,' he said, grinning. Then he was gone.

The next few days were similar. Mum was drinking most nights and each morning she would still be fast asleep on the chair. I tried to wake her to get her to go to work but she just shouted and lashed out, so in the end I just left her. One afternoon when Jake and I got home from school, my heart sank as soon as I opened the door. The air was thick with cigarette smoke laced with the strong smell of alcohol. There were three others in the living room: her friend, Eileen, and two men I'd never seen before.

'Shelley, Jake, how was your day at school?' Mum said with exaggerated interest. She staggered over and kissed us.

'I'll go and get Jake some tea,' I said, turning to go.

'No, no, I'm your mum,' she said, spitting the words out slowly and almost incoherently. '*I'll* go and get your tea!'

'Why don't you talk to your friends and let me do it?' I asked.

'I said I'd do it, so I will!' she shouted, taking very uncertain steps towards the door. She tripped over a can on the floor and, giggling hysterically, fell on top of one of the men.

'Why didn't you say you wanted to sit on my lap?' he said, and they all laughed loudly.

I took Jake's hand and we went into the bedroom. I was trying to avoid problems but, of course, it didn't work out that way.

A few minutes later she came into the bedroom. 'You're doing it again, Shelley, aren't you?'

'Doing what, Mum?'

'Trying to make my friends feel uncomfortable and make me feel guilty.'

'I'm not, Mum. I just want to get some tea and start on my homework.'

'Well, you can't! There isn't any milk. Go down to the shop and buy some. Here!' She threw some money at me.

'OK,' I said, reluctantly. 'Come on, Jake.'

'No, you leave him alone. I'll look after Jake.'

'But—' I started.

'No *buts*!' she yelled. 'Just go and buy some milk. I'm quite capable of looking after my own son!'

I wasn't sure. I could tell Jake wasn't either, but what could I say?

So I went down to the shop to get some milk. It takes about 10 minutes to get there but I ran most of the way so as to get back quickly. I expected noise and chaos when I opened the front door but to my surprise the flat was quiet. The sitting room was empty. I felt a momentary sense of relief, until I thought of Jake. I called. No answer. I went into the bedroom and kitchen – no sign of him. I sat down in the empty, stinking, sitting room, feeling cold and frightened. Monty came over and rubbed his head against my cheek. I'm sure he was trying to be helpful, but it didn't work. Where was Jake? Where had she taken him?

I couldn't think straight. I didn't know what to do. I phoned Joel. He was reassuring. He suggested I phoned Dad. I did. As I expected, he was beside himself with anger and came over straightaway.

'What should we do, Dad?' I asked.

'You stay here, in case Jake comes back on his own. I'll go out and start looking.'

About 10 minutes later he was back.

'The Polish guy next door saw your mum getting into a blue car with Jake and a couple of others,' he told me.

'But, Dad, they were all drunk. None of them was fit to drive!'

'I thought so,' he said. 'The trouble is, with a car they could be in any pub, anywhere. I don't know where to start!'

'Start with the local ones. That's where she usually goes.'

He grabbed his keys again.

'Can't I come with you?' I asked. 'I feel so useless here.'

'No, Shelley. Jake might come home on his own. Someone's got to be here.'

'Well, shall I phone the police?'

'I don't think they'll take any action. All we can say is he's gone off with his mum in a car. That doesn't amount to abduction. Tell you what. Phone Zandra and Fluff and ask them if they'll come and help.'

Zandra and Fluff arrived soon after. They'd deposited Marlon with a friend and were obviously anxious. They, too, set off on a tour of the local pubs. I was left alone, again with Monty. We paced the floor together.

It was a couple of hours later before all three of them came back. They'd seen no sign of Mum or Jake or the blue car. The evening went on like this. At about 10 o'clock Dad phoned the police. They were sympathetic and they put out a description to the local officers. We phoned Nan, Jake's friends, everyone we could think of. No one had heard or seen anything. Dad found out the addresses of some of Mum's friends – still nothing.

At about midnight, Dad was phoning the police again when we heard a key in the lock. We all rushed into the hall. It was Mum – but no Jake!

'Where's Jake?' shouted Dad.

'Isn't he here?' she said, staring round at us all.

'Of course not.' Dad grabbed her and shook her. 'Where did you take him, Liz?'

'Don't hurt me,' she wailed.

'Where is he?' Dad repeated, trying to control his fury.

'I don't know!' she shouted back.

I could see Dad going pale with anger. Zandra moved in between them and spoke calmly to Mum.

'Liz,' she said, taking her by the arm. 'Tell us where you took Jake.'

'We went to someone's house. Tommy's house, and we stayed there for a while. Jake was all right. He played with a little cat there.'

It was difficult to make out what she was saying. She was sobbing so violently.

'Then we went to a pub near Tommy's house. Jake didn't want to come. I got cross with him but he wouldn't come. He said he'd stay and play with the cat.'

'And then what?' asked Zandra.

'When we got back, he wasn't there. I thought he must have come home, so I came back and . . .' she burst into hysterical weeping.

'Liz, where is Tommy's house?' Zandra continued.

'I don't really know. It's somewhere in Camberwell.'

'Camberwell!' I repeated, horrified. 'Jake won't know his way home from Camberwell.'

We all stared at each other in rising panic. Dad got straight on the phone to the police. Within about 10 minutes they were there, questioning Mum. She was trying to remember Tommy's second name but couldn't. She described the street, the house and the pub – they could have been anywhere.

Dad was trying all her friends to try and get an address. Fluff had gone back to the local pubs to try and track down Tommy or someone who knew him.

It was an hour or so later when the WPC who stayed with us had a call. They'd found Mum's friend Eileen and she knew Tommy's phone number. The police were on their way to the address.

I was feeling totally helpless. I thought writing this letter might calm me down but it hasn't. I'm feeling colder and colder, more and more numb by the minute. I know Jake better than anyone. What would he have done? As soon as Mum and her friends went to the pub Jake would have tried to phone or get home. He hasn't got any money. He's never been on a bus alone. His sense of direction is awful and he'll be so frightened.

Horrible, terrifying thoughts are filling my mind. I've heard so many stories of missing children. I keep having to force myself not to think these things. Jake is going to be all right. Jake is going to be all right.

I'll finish this letter now. Fluff said he'll post it when he goes on another search. I'm so frightened, Ziggy.

Love,
Shelley

To Shelley,
Thinking of you.
Praying for Jake.

Love
Ziggy

Shelley Wright

16 Waterstone House

London SE6

THE ROUGHEST GAME

One step forward,
Two steps back
One slip sideways,
You're off the track
Ain't life the roughest game
Ain't life the hardest road

June 1

Dear Ziggy,

Thanks for your card. My main news is that Jake was found! Nothing else is really important but I'll tell you what happened.

All that night we sat around, went out searching, and phoned everyone we could think of. I spent most of the time making tea for friends, family, neighbours and police.

By the morning we had no news. Everyone was looking grim. The police were trying to be cheerful, telling us about children who'd gone missing and then turned up alive and well.

As soon as it was light they organised a huge search of the streets near Tommy's house in Camberwell. I joined in because Nan was at home manning the phone. When the officer gave us all our instructions, I was nearly sick.

'You must check everywhere – bins, cars, drains, gardens, kennels, sheds, under sheds, under cars, etc. You must look inside all carrier bags, black bin bags, fertiliser bags and sacks.'

He didn't say so but we all knew he meant we may find, not Jake, but his body. I gritted my teeth and searched. Loads of people had volunteered to help. I remember checking all sorts of unlikely places. All I could hear was people calling his name.

Then, as Zandra and I were going through some little park we suddenly heard a cheer. We looked at each other and rushed towards the sound. We could see from the smiles on everyone's face that the news was good. A WPC rushed over to me.

'We've found Jake,' she said.

I promptly burst into tears.

'Where is he?' asked Zandra, holding onto my hand tightly.

'He's at home,' she said, beaming.

We didn't wait to hear any more. We dived into

Zandra's car and belted home. The door was wide open. There were people everywhere. Inside, Jake sat between Nan and Dad, cuddling Monty and looking dazed.

'Are you all right?' I asked.

'Yes, I'm just a bit tired,' he said.

'Where were you?'

'On a bus,' he answered.

Typical Jake. He always was a boy of few words. Dad saw my puzzled expression and explained.

'He left Tommy's house to try and get home. He had £1 that one of your mum's friends gave him. He found a bus stop and caught a bus. Then he seems to have just gone to sleep. When he woke up the bus was in the garage and everything was dark so he didn't dare move. He waited until morning and then asked at the garage which bus he should catch to get home and – hey presto – he arrives on the doorstep.'

'Oh Jake!' I laughed and gave him a big hug.

It was a great day. Dad took Jake and me, Joel, Zandra, Fluff and Marlon out for a pizza. We had a great time. When we got home I was wondering where Mum had got to. She'd disappeared as soon as Jake came home. Then, as soon as I walked in I saw she'd been busy. She'd cleaned and tidied everything, bought flowers, bought lots of food and put a little beanie puppy on each of our beds.

It was the start of another of Mum's big battles against the booze. She managed a whole week without touching a drop and being the perfect mum. But it was Saturday nights she always found hard. She worked all day on the market stall and Jake and I went to the cinema with Joel and his brother. (I hardly dare let Jake out of my sight since the night he disappeared.) When we came home, about 8 o'clock, she was out. At 9 o'clock we got our daily check-up call from Dad. (He's nervous too!) She still wasn't back so I guessed she must have given in to temptation. I went to bed, only to be woken up by the phone ringing. It was the police.

'This is PC Granger, love. I'm afraid your mum's got herself into a bit of bother again. Is your dad there?'

'Not at the moment. What kind of bother?'

'There was a bit of a fight in the club she was in and—'

'Is she hurt?' I demanded.

'Only a few cuts and bruises. That's not the problem. The thing is, the woman she was fighting with wants to file assault charges. That puts us in a difficult situation since your mum's already on bail.'

'What are you going to do?'

'We'll have to keep her here tonight. Tomorrow, she'll be charged and then a decision will be made about her breaking bail.'

There was a silence.

'Do you understand, love?'

'Yes, yes thanks,' I said and rang off.

I was once again in a state of panic. But uppermost in my mind was the thought that if Mum went to prison, they might try to take me and Jake into care. I rang Dad and he came round immediately. It was just as well. Soon after he arrived there was a ring at the door.

A male PC, a female PC and another woman arrived. I think they were all a bit surprised to see my dad. I was so relieved he was there. They couldn't take us away if Dad was there.

'We just came round to check the children were all right,' said the WPC, smiling at me.

'Well, as you can see, Shelley's upset and Jake is fast asleep.'

'Of course you're upset,' said the woman. 'I'm Linda. I'm the Duty Social Worker. The police asked me to come along in case we needed to accommodate the children.'

'What do you mean?' asked Dad.

'I mean, to look after them while their mother's not here,' Linda continued.

'I can do that!' said Dad angrily.

'Of course,' said Linda. 'But you must see why the police were concerned. After all, it was only a week or so ago that Jake disappeared. You obviously weren't looking after him then!'

It was a vicious thing to say.

'That happened when their mother was meant to be in charge of him. Neither Shelley nor I were here!'

'Precisely,' said Linda.

'Look,' said Dad. 'I don't know what you're suggesting. We all know that their mum sometimes gets a bit drunk and does irresponsible things but I don't see why that should mean they need "accommodating".'

'Well, we have a duty to make sure they're not neglected—'

'Neglected! Of course they're not neglected!'

'What about tonight? Who was looking after them tonight?'

'Hang on,' I said. 'It's quite legal for me to be left in charge of Jake. That's not against the law and it's not neglect.'

'It could be seen that way,' she went on. 'However, tonight isn't the problem. What will happen if their mother is imprisoned?'

'Then I'll look after them,' said Dad, putting his arm around me protectively. 'Look, these two have lots of people who will take care of them. You don't need to worry. Tonight, I'll stay here. Tomorrow, when we know what's happening I'll make arrangements for them to live here under the care of an adult or I'll take them to my house or their grandmother's. Does that satisfy you?'

Linda looked Dad in the eye, then looked at me.

'Yes, it does,' she said categorically, then turned to me. 'Shelley, I'm sorry to have disturbed you. I hope things work out well. Goodnight.'

And off they went.

The following day we found out that Mum was going to be kept on remand because of the seriousness of the charge. It was GBH (grievous bodily harm!). We also discovered the name of the woman who was making the charge. It was a woman called Jean Fox. I'd never heard of her but Joel had. She was a friend of Janice's mum.

Thank goodness it was half-term so I didn't have to confront Janice yet – but I couldn't get the situation out of my mind. Somehow, that family was poisoning us.

Of course there was a big family meeting to decide what was going to happen to Jake and me. The decision was that Nan would come to stay with us Monday to Thursday and we would go to Dad's every weekend. No one has any idea how long Mum's going to be in prison.

We're allowed to visit her once a week. I hate it. We sit in a big room, like a café, all at separate tables. There's warders watching. I was terrified the first time we went. Some of the other prisoners looked really nasty and the warders look ready to attack at any moment. There was a big row and the warders had to break it up.

The next time it was quiet and boring. I do quite like watching some of the other people there. There's one huge, completely bald woman who has thousands of earrings, nose rings and eyebrow rings. She looks frightening but Mum said she's really quiet and kind. Then there's a woman with masses of blonde hair piled up on her head and tattoos everywhere. She's got two different men who visit her, Dave and Stan. I noticed that she always has the correct name on her tattooed arms. Mum told me that really she's got *Tom* tattooed there but she covers it up with some special stuff and puts a transfer with the right name on top!

Mum cried all the time during our first visit. But since then she's tried to smile and be cheerful. She wants to know everything we've been doing. She doesn't like telling us about what she does. It's awful leaving her there at the end of the visit. I can't bear to think about what her life is like in there.

Anyway, as you see life remains eventful for me. I'm getting used to the new situation. And everyone's been really kind, especially Joel and his family. I'm still lucky in some ways.

Lots of love,
Shelley

Shelley
You're amazing!
Hang on in there.

Love
Ziggy

Shelley Wright
16 Waterstone House
London SE6

DESPAIR

This despair I feel
It's a prison cell
It's a deep, dark mine
It's a doorless room
I think I've fallen
Into a black black hole

June 15

Dear Ziggy,

Thanks so much for the card. I don't know why you said I was amazing, I only wish I was. I realised how un-amazing I was this week because we had Sports Day. I've always thought of myself as being quite good at sport, but I think it's only because I'm tall and always been able to get the ball before other people. So Sports Day was a bit of an eye opener. I came fifth out of six in the 200 metres, so I obviously can't run very fast. I came tenth out of twelve in the high jump, so I can't jump. I wasn't allowed near the javelins and I wasn't good enough to go in for throwing the rounders ball. So, my idea of myself as reasonably fit and athletic died a bit of a humiliating death.

As you know, I was dreading the return to school because of Janice. I had good reason. As soon as I walked into the form room on the first day of term, she confronted me.

'So, Shelley, are you still proud of your mother?'

I pushed past her and sat down next to Leonie.

'Don't you ignore me!' she shouted.

'Leave her alone, Janice,' said Leonie.

'Why? Her mother didn't leave Jean Fox alone. Or haven't you heard? Her mum's in the nick now. Not only is she a drunk but she's a violent drunk. She goes around attacking innocent people in clubs. Don't try to deny it, Shelley. I know. My mum was there! Jean's her friend.'

I didn't know what to do or say. I know I wanted to punch her in the mouth – but of course that would just make me the violent daughter of a violent drunk. Leonie grabbed my arm very firmly so I couldn't stand up.

'Look, Janice, Shelley's been through a lot recently. I think you should show some sympathy, not make things even worse!'

'Been through a lot! Huh! I don't think your

precious friend's been too down. She's been parading around with her boyfriend, not weeping into her pillow.'

'Janice, why are you doing this?' I asked, speaking very carefully.

'Doing what? You mean telling people the truth about you?'

'No, I don't mean that. Ever since I arrived in this school you've been out to get me. Why?'

Janice stared at me.

'Oh, don't flatter yourself, Shelley! I have no particular interest in you.'

'Nor has anyone else,' I said quickly. 'So why do you tell them my business?'

'Because your business seems to involve people being beaten up, and stealing other people's boyfriends.'

This was unexpected.

'Are you talking about Joel?' I asked in some surprise.

'Of course I am. Or have you got other boyfriends?'

'Well, who am I meant to have stolen him from?'

She didn't answer.

'Are you saying I stole Joel from *you*?' I said,

incredulous.

'Of course you did!' she said.

'Well, I think he'll be surprised to hear that,' I said.

She looked a bit uncomfortable. She was about to say more but our teacher came in. I thought about it. Janice had always claimed to have boyfriends but I'd never listened very carefully to what she said about them. Maybe it had all been lies to make herself seem more worldly and grown-up. Maybe she'd always wanted to be Joel's girlfriend. The thoughts chased round in my head. At least talk of Joel had put Mum's crimes out of Janice's and everyone else's mind for a while.

After that, Janice seemed subdued. Leonie thought she was plotting something. I was just relieved she'd stopped making the comments. A few quiet days went by, then something odd happened.

As I walked out of school one afternoon, an older boy, who must have been about 19 or 20, came up to me.

'Hi, Shelley,' he said. 'Joel sends his love.'

'Thanks,' I said. 'Who are you?'

'The man with no name,' he said and winked at me. He then strode over to a very expensive car and it drove off. I realised that he and I had been the focus of some attention. Later, I described him to Joel. He didn't recognise the description at all. I was really puzzled.

It happened again a couple of days later. This time I tried to stop him to ask who he was. He slipped away but I did write down the car's registration number. Joel didn't recognise that either.

The next time he approached me his line was different.

'Hi, Shelley, Joel asked me to give you this.' He held out his hand.

'What is it?' I asked.

He grinned. 'Just a little present!' he said, and pushed a little packet towards me.

'What is it?' I asked.

But he was gone. The packet had fallen on the ground. I picked it up. It was a tiny plastic packet with a lump of something brown inside.

'What on earth—?' I said.

'Oh, my God,' said Hazel. 'It's drugs! It's heroin or cocaine or something!'

We all stared at it.

'Don't be stupid, Hazel. It can't be heroin or cocaine,' said Leonie, poking it. She opened the packet and sniffed it. 'It's draw. Cannabis.'

'Are you sure?' asked Hazel.

'Yes. I've seen it lots of times.'

'But why did he give it to me?' I demanded, feeling suddenly sick.

'He said it was from Joel,' Hazel reminded me.

'But it isn't,' I protested. 'Joel doesn't know him and Joel doesn't do drugs.'

'Well, who's it from, then?'

We stared at each other. A clammy kind of fear hit me. There was something weird and disturbing going on that I couldn't grasp. I looked around and realised that my unexpected gift had attracted quite a bit of attention from other girls leaving school.

'I don't like this one little bit,' I said. 'This is some kind of trick!'

'I don't like it either,' agreed Leonie. She was as worried as I was. 'Get rid of it!'

'Where?' I asked, looking round.

'Down the drain!' said Hazel.

Without any further thought I dropped the little packet down a drain. We were silent for a while, staring after it and aware that a whole group of girls were staring too.

'I don't think we should have done that, you know,' said Leonie thoughtfully.

'Why?' I asked, as unsure as she was.

'I think we should have taken it to the police!'

'Yeah, I think you may be right,' I agreed. 'But what can we do now? It's gone.'

'Well, if he does that again we must go to the police!' she answered.

'I just want to know why he's doing this,' I said. 'Who is he? How does he know me? Who asked him to give me that stuff?'

I told Dad about it at the weekend but immediately regretted it because he drove straight round to Joel's house and interrogated him about this boy. But neither Joel, nor Leonie's brother nor any of their friends knew who the boy was.

'I think we should phone the police,' said Dad during supper on Sunday night. But the baby started screaming and he didn't get round to it.

And last Monday the world began to collapse completely. At break, I realised I'd lost my locker key. I asked round the class and in the office but it hadn't been seen. By that time it was the end of break, so I had to go to my science lesson. I was going to have another search at lunchtime. Then about halfway through the lesson, the Deputy Head, Miss Tiptree, came in and asked me to come with her. She said nothing as we walked briskly down to the Head's office. I was getting more and more scared as we walked. I'd never been in the Head's office. I couldn't begin to imagine what had happened. Inside, the Head sat behind her big black desk looking grim.

'Come and sit down here, Shelley,' she said, indicating a chair. Miss Tiptree stayed, towering ominously behind me.

'I'm afraid I have something extremely serious to discuss,' she began. 'This morning I received some disturbing information about you.'

'Is this about my mum?' I asked, thinking she'd heard that Mum was in prison.

'No, Shelley. This is about you. I was informed that you have been known to bring drugs on to the school premises.'

My mouth fell open. 'What?' I said incredulously.

'I was incredulous too,' she continued. 'But I was informed that there was some persuasive evidence. On several occasions a young man, who is known to have connections with the drugs world, has been seen approaching you outside school. He seems to know you. He certainly knows your name.'

What is going on? I thought.

'But I—'

'Wait. I'll give you a chance to explain yourself in a minute. To continue. I was informed that he has been seen outside school giving you packets containing drugs.'

I was beginning to understand. There was some vicious plot behind all this.

'I found this disturbing enough, as you can imagine. But I was more alarmed when I was told that this morning you had brought drugs into school with the intention of taking them during the school day.'

'What?' I cried. 'This is ridiculous!'

'I sent Miss Tiptree to examine the contents of your locker. She had the school keeper break the lock and this is what she found.' She opened her desk drawer and brought out a little plastic bag with a brown lump inside, just like the one the boy had given me.

'Now, Shelley, what have you to say?'

I was too shocked to speak. I opened and closed my mouth like a fish, trying to speak and failing miserably. At last, I managed to get out a few hoarse, choking words.

'I think I know who's behind all this. Janice told you all this, didn't she?'

'I'm not going to tell you that, Shelley. Try to explain this to me, not shift the blame on to someone else.'

'OK, but you need to know that Janice has been out to get me from the moment I arrived in this school. Ask Miss McKenzie. Ask Miss Tiptree. And even more so now my mum's in prison for attacking a friend of her mum's.'

I saw a look pass over my head to where Miss Tiptree was hovering.

'It's Janice and her mum who have drug connections, not me. Ask other people. Ask my boyfriend's family. They'll tell you!'

'I'm sure I'll be asking a lot of people a lot of things, Shelley, but right now I want to know just two things. One, is it true that a young man has given you packets of drugs outside school and, two, why was this in your locker?'

I felt complete panic. I was trapped. What could I say?

'The boy, the "young man", the one you're talking about, he's come up to me three times outside school. I don't know who he is or how he knows me. On the first two occasions he came up to me and said that Joel (that's my boyfriend) sent his love and then

200

disappeared before I could find out his name. It wasn't true. Joel's never met him. On the third occasion he came up and told me Joel had asked him to give me something. It was a packet like that.'

'And did he give it to you?' asked the Head.

'Yes. He pushed it at me.'

'And what did you do with it?'

'We threw it down the drain.'

'Why?' she asked.

'Because we were scared. We knew it was drugs and we knew it must be some kind of mistake or a trick. So I threw it down the drain. Afterwards, we realised it would have been better to keep it and take it to the police.'

'Indeed!' she said. 'You keep saying "we". Who is we?'

'Hazel and Leonie. There were lots of others around too.'

'And did Hazel and Leonie know about this as well?' she said, pointing to the little bag.

'Of course not. How could they? *I* didn't know about it.'

'Then how do you explain its appearance in your locker?'

'I lost my key this morning. Anyone could have

found it, or stolen it, and put something in there.'

I could see she was sceptical.

'I'm not lying. Anyone in my class will tell you I spent all the morning break looking for it. Ask in the office, I went there to see if it had been picked up!'

Another strange look went over my head to Miss Tiptree.

'Have you anything else to say?' asked the Head.

'Only that this is a set-up. And it's obviously Janice behind it.'

'Right. Miss Tiptree and I have listened to you and I will consider what you have said. However, my priority here is to deal with an immediate problem. Drugs have been found in your locker, Shelley. You know that this school has adopted a zero-tolerance policy on drugs. Our policy clearly states that anyone found in possession of drugs will be permanently excluded from school. There are no *ifs* or *buts* or special cases in this policy. I am therefore going to prepare the documents to permanently exclude you from school. Your father and your grandmother have already been informed. Your father is on his way from work to collect you from school. Do you understand?'

I understood nothing. My world had shattered.

Through all the problems I've gone through this year I've managed to keep myself calm – even when Jake was missing. But this was so outrageous, so unfair, so impossible. I sat like a statue. I was aware that both of them were speaking but I no longer heard anything. Some thread that kept me together had snapped.

Oh, Ziggy, I'm now existing in a permanent state of anger, helplessness and despair. I can see no way out of this.

Lots of love,
Shelley

Dear Shelley
Hang on in there.
Something will turn up.

Love
Ziggy

Shelley Wright

16 Waterstone House

London SE6

BELIEVE

After all that doubt
I suddenly found out
That you
Believe
In me

July 1

Dear Ziggy,
Your card was the brightest thing that's happened to me since the day I was sent home from school. I'm still in a state of numbness but I feel a bit more alive now. I'll tell you why.

That day, in that room, I realised that nothing I could say would change the Head's mind. I'd been charged, tried and found guilty before I even entered the room. What broke the spell was my dad. He stormed into the school, and despite the secretary trying to stop him, he marched into the Head's office and told her how outrageous the whole thing was. He told her she should be ashamed of condemning me so quickly and that he'd prove my innocence and when he did he wanted a full apology! The Head and Miss Tiptree tried to calm him down but he wasn't having it. He grabbed my arm and marched me out. We sat in the car and he made me tell him all the details. He then drove me straight to the police station to ask them what charges could be filed against Janice. I could see the police didn't take it too seriously but they took notes and promised to get back to him.

I felt so much better knowing that he believed in me. Then, later, Nan and Joel reacted just the same. Not a moment's doubt. So I felt a bit better in one way but my position remained the same, despite Dad's determination to clear me. He began a thorough campaign. He gathered statements and evidence from everyone he could think of – all my classmates, Joel, Joel's parents, Joel's friends. He asked the school to provide a statement from Miss McKenzie, my Head of Year and Miss Tiptree about their knowledge of Janice's behaviour towards me. All this was great but the fact was they had found drugs in my locker and I had been seen accepting drugs from a boy outside school – and that's all they needed.

The governors' meeting to decide on my exclusion

was coming up. I could see there would be a huge argument but I couldn't see the governors disagreeing with the Head, especially as the Chair of Governors is known to have extreme views on drugs. From what I've heard he thinks cigarette smokers should be executed, let alone people who take illegal drugs!

Then the evening before the meeting I had some news that could help me. I had the most frantic phone call from my friend Hazel. You may remember that ages ago I mentioned a girl called Cheryl, who Janice always picked on and who left the school after Janice accused her of stealing. Well, Hazel met her and her mum. When she told them what had happened to me, they were really shocked – but they also thought they could help. Apparently, ever since that incident there's been a feud between the two families and Cheryl's mum has been trying to get the police to do something about Janice and her mum harassing their family. There wasn't enough evidence so Cheryl's mum decided to get the evidence herself. She'd paid her nephew to watch Janice's house, follow them and record anything that could be used against them. Some of the video tape showed Janice meeting a drug dealer and handing over money in return for packages. Hazel said she wasn't sure it could help but when she went round to see the tape she recognised the boy with Janice as the same one who approached me outside school. There are three tapes of Janice buying drugs. Each time the same boy is with her.

When I told Dad he was so excited! He raced round to Cheryl's house and asked her mum to come with us to the governors' meeting. We were allowed to have a friend with us – and she agreed. I was sure it wouldn't make any difference, they'd already made up their minds, but at least we had some evidence of Janice's connection with it all.

The morning of the exclusion meeting dawned. I'd hardly slept. I was terrified. At 7.30 the phone started ringing. All sorts of people phoned to wish me luck. At about 8 o'clock Joel came to the door with some flowers and a good luck card. At 9 o'clock Dad arrived. He looked like a lawyer. He was wearing a black suit, white shirt and grey tie. He had a shiny black briefcase. Inside, he'd photocopied little packs of documents and signed statements so that everyone at the meeting could have one.

Nan and Dad and I set off. We picked up Cheryl's mum on the way. I can't describe to you how awful it was driving up to school in those circumstances.

We were led into a conference room that I'd never seen before. There was a big table in the middle with several people already around it. We sat down and the Chair of Governors introduced himself and then everyone else. The Head was there with Miss Tiptree. There were three other people.

The Chair asked Miss Tiptree to put the school's case. She described how I'd been seen accepting drugs and she showed everyone the packet they'd found in my locker. Then the Head was asked to comment. She explained the school's zero-tolerance policy on drugs.

When I was asked about the allegations, I explained that I had been set up and that I wanted my dad to speak on my behalf. Dad stood up and opened his briefcase.

He told them he was going to show that I really was framed by Janice. One of the governors, who looked about a hundred years old, started tut-tutting. He kept muttering, 'Most irregular, most irregular.' It obviously annoyed Dad and he turned on him.

'If you wanted to find her guilty without listening to her side of the story then you shouldn't have bothered coming to this meeting,' he told him.

I held my breath. I thought they might tell Dad off

or say, 'You're right, we shouldn't have bothered,' but after a moment's silence the Chair just nodded for Dad to continue.

So Dad handed round the little packs he'd so carefully put together. They all stared at them in amazement. I don't think they expected my dad to be so organised. I was really proud of him, Ziggy, but it was a horrible moment. We had to sit watching while they looked through all the bits and pieces he'd put together. It seemed like hours.

Then, at last, the Head finished reading and put her copy of the pack back together. She thumped it on the table to straighten the edges. Everyone looked up at the noise.

'This does not prove Shelley to be innocent, Mr Wright,' she said. Her voice had a mean, icy edge to it and my heart sank. 'It may show that Janice has been unpleasant to Shelley but it's a big jump from being unpleasant to deliberately framing her in a criminal activity. And I'm afraid you have no evidence of that.'

I thought that was it. All Dad's hard work and faith in me had come to nothing. But I'd forgotten how stubborn my dad can be.

He told her that he did have evidence that

connected Janice directly to the drugs in my locker and the boy outside school. The Head looked at him in disbelief. The Chair looked at his watch impatiently. To cap it all the ancient governor started muttering 'Most irregular, most irregular' again. The Head smiled at Dad in a really patronising way and said, 'We all understand your desire to help your daughter, Mr Wright, but this is going a bit far.'

But Dad wasn't having any of it. He ignored the Head and told the Chair that he wanted them to listen to Cheryl's mother for just a couple of minutes. The Chair sighed, but then he agreed.

Cheryl's mum was so nervous, I could see her hands shaking. She told them who she was and how Janice had framed Cheryl for stealing money. She'd only been talking for a few minutes when the Head banged her hand on the table.

'This is not evidence about Shelley! This is a completely different business!' she said angrily.

'Please let me finish,' continued Cheryl's mum, rather less nervously, and went on without waiting for permission.

'The school decided, on that occasion, to blame my daughter and ignore Janice's part in it. But it led to a big argument between her family and mine.

Since then we've been continually harassed by both Janice and her mother—'

'This still isn't relevant!' said the Head even more angrily.

'But *this* is!' continued Mrs Browning firmly. 'The police said they couldn't do anything to stop Janice and her mother harassing us because there wasn't any real evidence. So I decided to gather the evidence myself. My nephew isn't in work right now, so I asked him to keep an eye on the two of them. I think he liked the idea of playing detective, so he's been following them about, videoing them.'

'Is that legal?' asked the Head.

'Is it legal to make someone's life a misery?' said Cheryl's mum. She seemed to have lost all her nervousness by then.

'Anyway,' she went on, 'these videos show that Janice is often with the boy who is meant to have given Shelley those drugs.'

'But that doesn't—' the Head began.

'Wait. I haven't finished,' said Cheryl's mum. I think the Head was a bit taken aback. She's not used to people interrupting her like that.

'The video also shows Janice and the boy buying packets of drugs, just like that one on the table, from a dealer who's well known in my neighbourhood.'

There was stunned silence.

'The video is here if you wish to watch it,' finished Mrs Browning.

The Head looked at the Chair of Governors. He looked at my dad.

'Have you any more surprises up your sleeve?' he asked.

'None at all, but I have already been to the police to make a complaint against Janice. When we leave here today we will be going to show the police all the things we've just shown you. When they've seen it I think they'll investigate Janice's activities a little more closely. And if *they* don't want to find the truth, we think the local press will.'

Very clever, I thought. I could see a little quiver run through the Head at the word 'press'. If there's one thing she doesn't like, it's bad publicity.

After that we were asked to leave so they could discuss it all. Miss Tiptree ushered us into a little waiting room. We were silent. The door opened and a secretary brought us some tea. We were silent again.

'Dad, whatever happens, you and Mrs Browning were great in there. I was really proud of you!' I said.

'Thanks, Shelley. Let's hope we were great enough

to sway them!'

We waited for about half an hour. Then Miss Tiptree came to take us back in.

'We have had a great deal of discussion on this matter,' said the Chair. 'Our final conclusion is this. We have decided that Shelley was probably not responsible for bringing drugs into school. So we will not be excluding her. This means Shelley may return to school on Monday.'

Had I misheard? I looked at Dad and Mrs Browning's faces. They were smiling. No, I hadn't misheard. I was not going to be expelled! I was so ecstatic, I hardly noticed what was going on. All I could think was *I've won, I've won*! After a minute or so I realised that Dad was still battling on. He was demanding an apology!

'I think that's going a bit far, Mr Wright,' said the Head. 'Don't push your luck!'

'I don't think *luck* comes into it,' said Dad, very grandly.

'I agree with Mr Wright,' said a small man who was from the Education Authority. 'You have my assurance that Shelley will receive an apology from both the authority and the school!'

The Head looked furious. I thought Dad would

stop there but he still wasn't satisfied.

'There's one more thing,' he said. 'What are you going to do with Janice?'

The Head looked meaningfully at the Chair of Governors. Both of them were obviously fed up with Dad.

'I will ask the Head to prepare the papers for her permanent exclusion,' said the Chair. 'And now, if there's nothing else, I will close this meeting.'

I was so happy when we left that room. Outside, there was a cluster of girls from my class, including Leonie and Hazel. They rushed over. When they heard the news they started shrieking with delight. Soon there was quite an uproar in the corridor. We moved outside quickly. We were just getting into the car when Miss McKenzie ran over.

'Shelley,' she said, smiling. 'I'm so pleased!' and she gave me a big, warm hug.

To cap it all, when we got home, Mum phoned to say her solicitor thinks she'll get bail at her court appearance next week, so she might be home soon.

You know I was dreading finishing this letter because I was convinced it would be all bad news and I'd be depressing you once more. Instead, I'm rushing to finish it so I can post it on the way to a big celebration and supper at my favourite Chinese restaurant. And I'm so excited!

Lots of love,
Shelley

Dear Shelley,
So pleased you won.

Love
Ziggy

Shelley Wright

16 Waterstone House

London SE6

BRIGHTER AND LIGHTER

The light
At the end
Of the tunnel
Is so much
Brighter
So much
Lighter

July 15

Dear Ziggy,
It was so nice to get your card. You really do read my letters, don't you? Well, I haven't really come down to earth yet. I was so sure I'd be expelled from school, I hadn't really dared think of anything beyond that meeting. I just knew it would be the end of my education, the end of my friendships and, worst of all, it would mean that Janice had won.

It took all weekend for me to realise that I really was going back to school. I was terrified. I thought Miss Tiptree and the Head would want to see me or that someone would tell me it was all a mistake. In fact, it was great. Janice's friends weren't there and everyone else in the class hugged me and congratulated me. I had to tell the story of the exclusion meeting over and over again. At lunchtime, all sorts of girls I'd never spoken to came up to me to say, 'Well done.' It was like being famous. Some of them also told me how mean Janice had been to them and I realised how many lives she'd been trying to wreck.

The most unexpected thing was the number of teachers who told me they were pleased I was back in school. In the afternoon, Miss Tiptree came up to me in the corridor. I thought she was going to make some nasty comment but she just said, 'Well done, Shelley. I'm very pleased.' I was amazed.

So, school's been great and home has been good too. Jake was really happy because he won a medal for the 100 metres in his school sports day (much better than me!) and Dad was there to see him. He's also going to get an IT prize at the end of term. It's the first time he's got anything like that and he still hasn't stopped smiling. Mum hasn't been granted bail yet, but the solicitor thinks she'll get it next week, in time for the summer holidays.

Talking of summer holidays makes me realise that

I've been writing to you for nearly a year now. You've sent me 22 postcards. I can hardly believe that. I didn't think you'd reply at all, you must get so many letters. And I never imagined you'd actually read what I wrote.

I want to thank you, Ziggy. It hasn't been all fun this year and my letters must have been pretty miserable some of the time. I just know it would have been much harder if I hadn't written it all down, and much, much harder without your postcards, which now cover half my bedroom wall. So, thank you. With a bit of luck, next year's letters will all be bright and happy.

Love,
Shelley

STAR

You made it
I always knew you could
You showed them
Like I knew you would
You really are
A star

June 30

Dear Shelley,

I think this is going to surprise you. It's a letter, not a postcard. I wanted to assure you that I really do read your letters. I'm so pleased everything turned out so well, but you really had me worried there for a while.

In your letter you thank me for my cards. You've got it wrong there, girl. It's me who should be thanking you for sharing so much with me.

I told you once that you're amazing, Shelley. It's true. You'd better believe it. You really are a star.

Love
Ziggy